About the Author

Verily Anderson has raised two Brownie Packs
in her time, one in the country and one in
London. She has been a Guide, Lieutenant,
Tawny and Brown Owl. She has worked on the
staff of *The Guide* and is a writer for and about
Brownies and Guides. She lives in Norfolk, has
four grown-up daughters and a son, and
twelve grandchildren!

Jacket illustration by Jenny Williams

THE BROWNIES AND THE CHRISTENING

Verily Anderson

Illustrated by Lesley Smith

KNIGHT BOOKS
Hodder and Stoughton

Text copyright © 1977 Verily Anderson
Illustrations copyright © 1977 Hodder and Stoughton Ltd

First published in 1977 by Hodder and Stoughton
Children's Books Ltd

Knight Books edition 1979

Printed and bound in Great Britain for
Hodder and Stoughton Paperbacks, a
division of Hodder and Stoughton Ltd.,
Mill Road, Dunton Green, Sevenoaks,
Kent (Editorial Office: 47 Bedford
Square, London, WC1 3DP) by
Cox & Wyman Ltd.,
London, Reading and Fakenham

ISBN 0 340 23476 8

Contents

1 · Wanted – a puppy

'It was terrible fun at Brownies today,' said Angela, 'wasn't it?'

'Super,' agreed Jean. 'Specially when we pole-jumped backwards and forwards across the stream.'

All the Brownies started to talk at once. Anybody might have thought it was a flock of chattering magpies instead of a pack of Brownies scampering over the Common.

'I liked building the bridge,' said Joey.

'And I laughed so much when Brown Owl and Tawny walked across it and Tawny nearly fell in, it gave me hiccups,' said Sassy.

'It may have been terrible fun for all of you,' Lucinda said more slowly, 'but I just thought it was terrible.'

'Brownies? Terrible?' They all started again. 'What's so terrible about making a fire to crowd round on a cold day?' 'With potatoes baked in the hot ashes to warm our hands?'

'Well, I just didn't like the way Tawny wore her skirt,' said Lucinda. 'It's at least six centimetres out of fashion. Brown Owl keeps on telling us how particular we've got to be about our uniforms, keeping them neat and ironed and clean, but she doesn't seem to have noticed that pockets just aren't *in* this year.'

'Pockets aren't meant to be in,' said Sassy. 'They're for putting things in.'

'Brownie uniforms are really meant to show that we're Brownies who can be useful if anybody needs us,' Tulip told her cousin Lucinda.

'And the badges on them show what sort of things we can be useful about,' the others joined in. 'Like First-Aider and Cook and Gardener.' 'And Hostess and Musician, and Toymaker and Friend to Animals. And the name-tapes on our shoulders tell which packs we belong to.' 'Yes, and Lela and Jennifer had to change their name-tapes when they went away and joined other packs.'

'And the brown belt is to hold us together, isn't it, Emma?' Angela asked her.

Emma had been a Brownie for over a year but had only lately come to live in the village. But just at this moment Emma was not thinking about Brownie belts. She was thinking about a brown dog-lead that was being pulled very tightly by the handle of the pram that Jean's mother was pushing and the collar round the neck of the fat eager little puppy giving welcoming yaps to the Brownies coming down the hill. Jean's mother bent down to let the puppy off the lead and Emma ran on in front to be the first to play with it. It came waddling up to her and she bent down to pick it up. What a little bundle of wagging tail it was! And it was not just its tail that wagged, but all of it, its nose and its ears and its whole wriggling warm little self.

'Dinky, Dinky,' Jean called it, and hearing its owner's voice the puppy leapt out of Emma's arms and raced off to Jean. But it was soon bounding about with all the Brownies and when Emma called 'Dinky', it came back to *her*.

'Oh, you are so lucky, Jean,' Emma said. 'If I had a puppy like this I'd love it more than anybody else in the world.' She thought for a moment. 'Next to my mother and father.'

'Then why don't you ask them to give you a puppy?' Lucinda said. 'Mine did when I wanted one. That's how I got Stephen. I just said I wanted a poodle and they bought me one.'

'Oh, Lucinda always has everything she asks for,' Tulip said of her cousin.

'Why not?' Lucinda said. 'I'm an only child. At least that's my mummy's excuse when other people say I'm spoilt.'

'I'm an only child too,' said Emma, 'but I don't have everything I want. I've asked and asked for a puppy but Daddy says we'd have to buy a licence and Mummy says she can't have a dog *and* a job.'

It was because of her mother's job that Emma always

went on to tea with one of the others after Brownies and after choir practice. On Sundays the friends came back to tea with her. Today it was with Sassy she was going home to tea. But she couldn't help wishing it were Jean, with her adorable, funny, sweet, cuddly little puppy.

'Dinky, Dinky,' she said stroking his ears. 'And what sweet little paws you've got. They're as soft and bouncy as marshmallows.'

'My dog likes *eating* marshmallows,' said Tulip.

'It's very bad for dogs' teeth to eat sweets,' said Amanda.

'And even worse for Brownies' teeth,' said Joey. 'Luckily my mother never gave me sweets at all when I was little. She gave me bits of apple and cheese instead. And I've never got around to liking sweets so I've never got around to having holes in my teeth either.' She opened her mouth to show how each tooth was white and perfect.

'My dog isn't allowed sweets and his teeth are perfect too.' 'My dog eats cheese but he doesn't eat apple.'

Everybody seemed to have dogs except Emma. Sassy had two.

'Come on, Emma,' said Sassy. 'We'll have to hurry if you want any tea, or the little ones will have eaten it all up.'

'What do you feed your dog on?' Emma said, as they turned off the Common together.

'Lady Lardy Cake likes the bits left over from the babies' plates and what they throw on the floor.'

'Lady *who*?'

'Lady Lardy Cake. That's what we christened our fussy dog. Our other dog, Buttered Toast, eats anything and everything,' said Sassy. 'He'll eat your shoes if you give him a chance. My brother Sam says leather is the same to a dog as meat. He says it's just dried up meat really, and I suppose he's right.'

Emma shuddered. The thought of walking about on pieces of dried up meat was not very nice. She was not really looking forward very much to seeing Sassy's twin brother Sam. He said such terrible things and thought up dreadful tricks to play on Sassy and her friends. And then there were all the other children. There were so many that she wondered how their mother could keep count. She would really rather have gone home and waited alone for her own mother to come home from work.

They reached the footpath that led along the riverside to the cottage. Small children were spilling out of the doors and windows and out into the garden. It was always like that at Sassy's, but so far there were no signs of Sam. Emma looked warily up into the trees to make sure he was not up one with a bagful of burrs to throw down on to them to cling to their caps and tangle up their hair. But it was getting dark and she could see nothing.

She hurried on after Sassy to get into the warm safe cottage as soon as possible. As they came in, Sam crawled out from under the table with a teddy bear in his mouth.

'I'm a lion,' he growled in a voice made gruffer by the bear's head half filling his mouth, 'and I eat children.'

The small owner of the bear gave an ear-piercing scream and tried to tug it out of her brother's mouth, but Sam just growled again and chased her into the wood basket.

Emma took off her coat and cap and hung them on a

peg with Sassy's and sat as far away from Sam as possible.

Sam was at his worst today. When he had finished teasing his little sister he put a sheet over his head and pretended to be a ghost. Now all the children began to scream and run away except Sassy who took no notice. Then everybody laughed except Emma. She knew there were really no such things as ghosts, but even to think about them spoilt the idea of the nice walk home in the dark with her mother.

Next, Sam went out of the room and suddenly there was a frightful crash as though a window had been broken. He gave a terrified yell and the children rushed to see what had happened. Emma followed them more slowly. Naughty as Sam was, she did not like the idea of finding him cut and bleeding from some dreadful accident. But Sassy did not even bother to get up. Then Emma saw the reason why. Sam had not broken a window at all. He had just thrown on to the stone floor a handful of small metal squares that made exactly the same sound as breaking glass. They all laughed again and then sat down to tea. Sassy's mother was big and fat and kind and kept on saying, 'Oh, Sam, do stop it,' all the time, just as though it were another way of breathing out. Only sometimes, instead of saying, 'oh, Sam, do stop it', she said, 'oh, Fred, do stop it', or 'oh, Kevin' or 'oh Dave' or 'oh Muriel' or 'oh, Ada', but never, today, 'oh, Sassy, do stop it'.

The Brownies and the christening

Sassy was much too helpful bringing in the bread and butter and heaving the smaller children up on to the benches each side of the long table. Emma tried to help too, but as soon as she put a toddler on to the bench, it slid off again and waddled away. Lady Lardy Cake was the only one who sat quietly waiting for tea to begin. Sam seemed at first to be helping too. He poured out some nice looking lemonade for everybody. But he was just going to take a drink out of his own glass when, to Emma's horror, she saw a huge worm swimming about in the glass. She screamed at him not to drink, but he took no notice and just took a huge gulp, narrowly missing the worm. Only when he had put his glass down did he pull the worm out and wave it in the air to show that it was really only made of plastic.

Emma was glad when tea was over and she could sit on the floor beside Lady Lardy Cake and stroke her ears. Some of the toddlers came and climbed all over her and Sassy's mother had to tell them not to.

'Poor old Lardy,' she said. 'Mind out or you'll hurt the puppies.'

'The puppies?' Emma exclaimed excitedly. 'Where are the puppies?'

'Inside Lardy Cake,' said Sam.

'You mean Lardy Cake is going to have puppies?' Emma said.

'Yes,' said Sassy, 'in two or three weeks' time. She has puppies every year – sometimes twice.'

'Then where are all the other puppies?' Emma asked, looking round hopefully.

'We find them kind homes,' said Sassy. 'We give them away.'

Emma's face lit up.

'Would you give me one?' she asked. 'I do dreadfully want a puppy.'

'But you said your mum and dad wouldn't let you have one,' said Sassy. 'They take a lot of looking after and if your mum's out at work, what would the puppy do all alone?'

And suddenly Emma began almost to cry. Here were puppies being given away, here was this nice warm cosy home full of children, even if they were noisy, and even if Sam was always playing pranks. And there was Emma, an only child like Lucinda, but with no dog and a mother with a job.

When Emma's mother arrived to take her home, although she knew it would be no good, Emma started off at once, in front of all Sassy's family, saying: 'Mummy, please, please, please, let me have a puppy. Lady Lardy Cake is going to have lots and Sassy says they give them away. I could take the puppy to school and look after it there.'

'No, you couldn't,' said Sam. 'I've tried often. They make you take it home.'

'Then can't you change jobs for one you can take a dog to?' Emma asked her mother.

'You don't want your mum to work in a circus do you?' said Sassy's mother, smiling. 'How would you like to see her walking the tightrope? Wouldn't you be afraid she might fall off?'

'Yes, I would,' said Emma, getting the same feeling again as when Sam had nearly drunk the worm. 'There must be some kind of job a dear little puppy could go to. It could stay quietly under the counter in a shop.'

'Puppies don't stay dear little things,' said Sassy's mother. 'They grow. Look at Lardy – she was only little once.'

Emma looked at Lady Lardy Cake. She had stretched and stood up and Emma saw at once that a dog her size would not even fit very easily into her mother's kitchen, let alone under a counter in a shop.

'Emma's always going on about wanting a puppy but our flat's too small,' Emma's mother said. 'Oh well, it's time we went off into the dark, Emma.'

2 · Explosion children

Next week at Brownies, Brown Owl asked everybody to bring a toy she had outgrown for the children who had lost everything in a terrible factory explosion that had wrecked their homes. Most of the Brownies had seen, on television, scenes of this dreadful disaster in the north of England, with a row of houses looking like nothing more than a few piles of rubble and broken sticks. Among it all, they had been told, were half a dozen homes with beds, chairs, tables and everything in them completely smashed up. The children of that row were all at school when the chemicals in the nearby factory exploded. But three of the fathers had been killed in the factory and two of the mothers in their homes.

'Think how lonely those children must be,' Brown Owl said. 'Their homes gone! And their toys, and some, their best things of all, their fathers and mothers!' . . .

'I know you'll each want to bring your very newest toy that has most lately been given to you, but that might hurt the feelings of the person who gave it to you. It would give just as much pleasure to a lonely child if you gave a toy you have had for quite a long time, and grown very fond of, but don't play with very often now.'

'But I'd love to give a lonely child my new tea-set,' said Angela. 'I'm sure Mummy wouldn't mind although I play with it every day. She'd be glad I was doing a really good deed.'

'Well, I'd hate to give away any of my new toys,' said Lucinda. 'Not that my mother and father would mind. They'd just buy me some more.'

This week Emma was going to have tea with Angela. Angela's mother came out to greet the two Brownies as they arrived at her gate.

'And have you told Emma about our lovely surprise?' she said and Angela shook her head. 'No, we were talking about Brownie things and I forgot,' she said.

'Forgot your surprise?' her mother said. 'What would you do if I forgot you?'

Angela turned to Emma.

'It's a new baby we've got,' she said.

'Boy or girl?' Emma asked politely. She had seen rather a lot of babies lately. There were all those toddlers at Sassy's and then there was something squeaking away in the pram that Dinky was attached to. A new puppy would have been a surprise. But babies, as far as she knew, were not particularly interesting. They went indoors and Emma saw the cot in the corner of the room. Angela took her over to it and if they both stood on tiptoes they could see over the edge. The baby was asleep. It looked like the doll she had had for ages, whose eyes flopped shut as soon as she lay it down. Emma had once tried to wash its face and after that it shrank. The baby's face looked just as putty-coloured and shrunk and it did not seem to be breathing. The mother looked at it too and seemed not to mind that it was so dull. How cuddly a puppy would have looked, all curled up and asleep with its head tucked into its paws!

They went into Angela's room to talk about filling in their Brownie Pocket-books.

'I'm going to ask Tawny if I can draw and cut out two hands and stick them in my Red Pocket-book so I can colour one finger each day until someone passes my nails as really clean,' said Angela. 'I'll scrub my nails with a nail brush and if my mother says they are perfect I'll paint one nail blue on the chart I make.'

Emma's Red book was all filled in and now she was on to the Brownie Road with a Brown Pocket-book. She turned to page eight where she had to write down three occasions when it can be difficult to obey quickly. She said: 'I'm going to ask Brown Owl or Tawny if I can fill them in as: One, playing with Dinky. Two, looking in an animal shop window with some puppies in it. Three, seeing Lady Lardy Cake's family for the first time.'

After tea the baby woke up and yelled. The noise

was almost unbearable but nobody seemed to mind. It sounded like a cogwheel that needed oiling that went round and round making the same rasping noise, each time at the same place. Emma was glad when her mother came to fetch her home.

'I really think,' she said to her mother, 'babies are the worst things. They're so boring and so ugly and they make such a dreadful noise.'

Her mother laughed.

'You were a baby once yourself,' she said.

'Oh, I know,' Emma said, 'and so were you too. And Daddy. But the good thing is you aren't now.'

Emma told her mother how the Brownies were going to give toys for the explosion children to cheer them up.

'Would it hurt your feelings if I sent the baby doll you and Daddy gave me one Christmas?' Emma asked her mother.

'No, but won't you miss her?'

'Not in the least,' said Emma. 'And some poor child who has lost her father or mother in the explosion might quite like babies.'

3 · Promises! Promises!

Soon it was fine enough to have Brownies out-of-doors in the wood. They could see so many promises of spring that Brown Owl said they had better make up a song together about everything they could see and hear and smell that promised the spring.

As they came down the hill across the Common, some of them began to sing snatches of the song they had made up to a tune that was a mixture of Top-of-the-Pops and Brownies' Singing Games and Church Hymns.

'The sticky horse chestnut buds promise to turn into green fingers – look how the green spikes are poking up from the ground promising to be bluebells,' they warbled. 'Newly scratched-up earth by the burrows promises baby bunnies scampering' – 'lovely little green leaves in the brown earth promise to be prim-roses' – 'a thrush singing on a high branch promises a nest of speckly eggs' – 'that promise to hatch out into cheepy little fledglings,' they sang.

All these promises had been kept, by the time it was

The Brownies and the christening

Angela's turn to have Emma to tea again. Spring had really come. It was after choir practice, which Brown Owl always took as well as taking Brownies. This week Brownies would be on Saturday morning.

Emma and Angela came running through the rectory garden together, humming little bits of the psalm they had been practising. 'Oh clap your hands together all you people,' and they clapped their hands together above their heads and to the right and to the left, as they did in a Pack Salute when they wanted to say 'Welcome' or 'Thank you' or 'Well done'.

Then they clapped their hands behind their backs, and then they clapped each other's hands. It was great fun.

As they came to Angela's gate, Emma suddenly remembered the baby, and she could understand now how easy it was for Angela to have forgotten about it before. But once they were inside the gate, it was Emma who was forgotten. Angela went rushing in to see her baby brother as though they had been parted for months. She peeped into the cot but to Emma's relief he was not there. The thought of that pale ugly face that would soon burst out into a squall was not very cheering.

They heard Angela's mother call to them from the garden where she had tea ready for them under the apple tree. Emma followed Angela out. There was a rug on the ground which Angela flung herself on to excitedly. And there, when Emma joined her, was a most amazing

sight. Instead of the shrivelled-up little pallid thing
she had seen before was a big gurgling chubby pink and
white creature with all the adorable funniness of a
puppy. She knelt down to look at it more closely and it
smiled up at her and chuckled. She held out one finger
and it curled its own little fat fingers round it and held
it tight. Angela did the same and now it had a Brownie's
finger in each fist. They bounced their hands up and
down in time and he bounced too, chuckling. What an
unbelievable change in only two or three months! 'Oh

clap your hands together,' they sang, and they clapped their hands and he loved it. Presently his mother gave him a rusk and first of all he examined it before he put it in his mouth.

'Is that all they eat?' Emma asked. 'Just puppy biscuits?'

'Oh no, he eats real food all mushed up and he eats it with a spoon and drinks masses and masses of milk.'

Emma watched in amazement as his mother took him on her knee and he opened his mouth with every spoonful ready to take it.

'He couldn't do that last time I saw him, could he?' Emma said.

'No, he does something new every day,' Angela told her.

'Babies do grow quickly,' Emma said, 'like puppies.'

'Puppies grow even quicker. Have you seen Dinky lately?'

'No, not for ages.'

'We can see into Jean's garden if we climb up the apple tree,' Angela said. 'He's usually playing about there now.' They both climbed up and Angela pointed down to the garden three houses away. Angela gave a call. Presently Jean came running out into her garden to answer it. With her was a large, leggy, gawky dog. He sniffed round a bit then lolloped over the fence to the next garden. 'Where's Dinky?' Emma asked.

'That *is* Dinky.'

'It can't be. It's a whole dog. Dinky's just a little roly-poly puppy.'

'I told you puppies grow quicker than babies.'

'And babies grow quickly enough,' Emma said, looking down again at Angela's baby brother. 'But I'm glad your baby hasn't turned into a great big whole full-sized man yet.' They both laughed.

'That will take a long time,' Angela said. 'About twenty years.'

'But I'm glad he's grown this much,' said Emma. 'I like him better like this.'

They went back to the rug to play with him again.

Meanwhile at home, Emma's mother had come home early. It was the last day of her job.

'The trouble is,' she was saying to Emma's father, 'Emma just hates babies. I don't know what we're going to do about it. She'll be so upset.'

'We'd better not tell her,' her father said.

'Oh, we must tell her. But how can we make her like the idea?'

'Wait till she sees the baby. She'll be pleased all right to have a baby of our own.'

Emma's mother shook her head. 'I'm afraid not,' she said. 'She saw Angela's baby brother and thought him terrible. She was so put off by the idea of babies she gave her baby doll away the next day.' She paused. 'She'd much rather have a puppy.'

Her father laughed. 'Yes, I'm afraid she would. She's always talking about wanting one.'

'Then perhaps we'd better let her have a puppy,' her mother said. 'Now I've given up my job I'd be able to look after it while she's at school.'

'A puppy and a new baby both at once!' her father said. 'Oh dear, that would be too much for all of us.'

'Just a very small puppy,' her mother murmured.

'What's the time?' Emma's father got up hurriedly.

'Nearly half-past six. It's time you went and fetched Emma from Angela's, but don't expect to find her in a very cheerful mood after hearing that baby yelling again.'

'The Post Office shop stays open late on Fridays,' he said. 'I know what we'll do. There's a wonderful-looking toy dog that's just come in. No little girl would be able to resist that, especially anyone who's so keen about dogs. We'll give her this dog when we tell her about the baby and then we can treat it just like a real dog and remind her when to feed it and brush it and take it out for walks. If she's really good at doing all that then we could think about getting her a real puppy later on.'

'There's only one thing wrong with that idea,' said Emma's mother. 'I've seen it too. It's not a toy dog, it's a nightdress case.'

They both burst out laughing.

'All the better,' Emma's father said. 'It will last her a lifetime.'

'And if it reminds her too much of the real puppy she wants,' her mother said, 'she can just open up the zip and keep her pyjamas in it.'

Emma's father reached the shop only just before it shut. The dog was still sitting on the counter, plumped up with paper inside it, as the post mistress explained when she turned it over and unzipped its tummy. When she took the paper out the fat cosy puppy with floppy ears and a short tail collapsed into a rather sad-looking bag.

'I've never seen a puppy with quite such pink ears in real life,' he said, 'but I don't suppose Emma will mind. I wonder what breed it is?'

'Most breeds look the same when they're puppies,' said the shop lady. 'It could be a Pomeranian and then again it might be a Great Dane.'

'I'd rather it wasn't a Great Dane,' Emma's father said. 'Our kitchen isn't very big.'

'Will you take it just like this or shall I stuff the paper back?'

'Oh, put the paper back,' Emma's father said, 'and more besides. We want it to be a really wonderful present. It doesn't look much, all floppy like that.'

So together they stuffed it out, puffed it up and tweaked it here and there till it looked really puppy-like.

27

'Now we need a collar and lead,' Emma's father said. 'And a dog bowl and a dog brush, and a rubber bone – in fact everything but a dog licence.'

'We shall be having some dog baskets in later on,' said the post mistress. 'Maybe you'd like one of those too?'

'Yes,' said Emma's father. 'I'll come in again when you've got one.'

The post mistress made everything into a big parcel. It all took so long that he was already late for collecting Emma. She would probably want to know what was in the parcel, but he would keep it a secret till they got home and her mother broke the news to her about the new baby.

4 · *Surprise! Surprise!*

Emma's father reached Angela's house to find that her mother had already taken Emma home.

'It was a lovely evening for a walk with the pram,' said Angela's mother, 'and I thought we might meet you on the way.'

Poor Emma! She had probably not been able to bear another minute with the bawling baby and had asked to go home early! Her father followed her.

There was nowhere in their small flat where he could hide the parcel properly so he decided that the news must be broken as soon as he got back. First they would give her the puppy and while Emma was playing with it they would just mention the expected baby as though in passing. He could hear Emma clattering about in the garden when he got back. Carefully he unwrapped the puppy and put the collar and lead on it and stood it by the kitchen table, with the dog bone in front of it, and the dog brush beside it. He filled the dog bowl with water and put it down by the table too.

'Oh, it really does look life-like,' said Emma's

29

mother. 'If only its ears weren't quite so pink, it might be a real puppy.'

They both went out into the garden.

Emma was practising walking along upturned flower-pots. She stood on two and then bent down to move another one so that she could step on to it as though she were crossing a fast stream on movable stepping stones.

'Emma,' her mother said. 'You know how you've always said you so terribly wanted a puppy? Well—'

Emma stood up straight on the flowerpots.

'I know I've always said I wanted a puppy,' she said, 'but I don't want us to have a puppy now. What I really want us to have is a baby.'

Her mother and father exchanged surprised glances.

'It's too late to take it back,' her father said.

'Take what back?' Emma asked.

'It's a sort of joke Daddy's bought you,' her mother said, 'a present, for fun.' She gave Emma's father a look that meant, 'Go on. You tell her now.'

'But it's not my birthday,' Emma said.

'No, but in the summer it will be somebody else's birthday and so it's a good moment for a present when we tell you about it,' her father said.

'Somebody else's? Whose birthday?' Emma asked.

'Your little baby brother or sister. Mummy's going to have a baby in the summer.'

'Oh! Oh! Oh!' Emma cried with excitement and joy and she hopped off the flowerpots. First she hugged her father, and then she hugged her mother and they all laughed so much they all nearly fell over.

'Mind you don't squash our baby,' her mother said, as Emma hugged her again.

'Is our baby already there inside, like Lady Lardy Cake's puppies?' Emma asked. 'Oh, how lovely! We must take great care of it. We must get all ready for it. Oh, I am so happy.' She turned two cartwheels on the grass to show how happy she was. 'I wish we were going to have it today. I'll never be able to wait till the summer.'

'Well, there's always this present to be going on with,' her father said. 'Come and see what you think of it.'

They all went into the kitchen.

'Oh, isn't he adorable?' Emma said admiringly, but instead of leaving him on the floor and pulling him along on all fours on his lead, she picked him up and turned him over and cradled him in her arms like a baby.

'There, there,' she said. 'Don't cry. It's nearly time for your next feed.'

'What are you going to give him?' asked her father. 'A bone? And some puppy biscuits?'

'Oh no,' Emma said. 'First of all some sieved vegetables with a teaspoon and then he can finish up with his bottle.' She took the collar and lead off and laid it on the table, then fetched a little shawl to wrap him in and tucked him down in her doll's cot.

31

Her father and mother looked at each other again. This time they both started laughing out of sheer relief. Her father picked up the collar and lead, the dog bone and the brush.

'Maybe you'd rather I changed these at the shop for a baby's bib and a feeding bottle?' he asked Emma.

'Oh yes, Daddy, and he really ought to have a proper nursery safety-pin for his nappies.'

Next day, Emma's mother opened a drawer in her room that Emma had never looked into before, and brought out some of the clothes that Emma had worn when she was a baby, to wash and iron them all ready for the next one.

'I made these little nighties for you and this little dress,' her mother said.

'Oh, aren't they super!' Emma cried. 'Won't our baby look ducky in them?'

Emma held up a little sleeping suit. 'But this is much too big for a new baby,' she said.

'It started off as small as you were,' her mother said, 'and then it stretched and grew with you. We shall have to start again with a new growy for our new baby.'

'Maybe we could change the dog collar and lead at the shop for a growy for my baby puppy?' Emma asked.

'Except that he won't grow like a real baby,' her mother said, laughing.

'Oh, yes, he will,' said Emma. 'I've taken some of the stuffing out and then I'll put it back slowly to make his growy stretch like a real baby's. The paper that was so crumpled up inside him was rather rustly so I put some of my socks in him instead.'

'That's all right if you don't lose them,' her mother said, 'or forget where they are.'

'Lose my darling new baby puppy? Of course I shan't. You're not going to leave our new baby lying about and forget where he is are you?' She paused and then asked: 'Mummy, do you think my new baby puppy could borrow one of the nighties till he's got a growy of his own?'

Her mother picked out one with daisies sewn all round the collar.

'He'd better have this blue one as he's a boy. It will go nicely with his pink ears,' she said.

Emma eased him into it and he looked much more like a real baby, specially when she tied on a woollen bonnet, which her mother found for her to keep his ears warm. Then she helped her mother to wash the other baby clothes, squeezing the little woollies gently through the soap suds in water that was not too hot and not too cold and then rinsing them in water of exactly the same temperature. Then they rolled the woollies up in a towel to squash the water out without hurting the delicate fibres by wringing them. They spread them out flat to dry on another towel in an airy place in the kitchen that was not too hot and not too cold either.

Emma got out her Brown Pocket-book and made a note on a piece of paper to ask one of her Brownie Guiders if she could fill in the page called *Brownies help at home* (page 16): '*Make a list of the way you have helped clothes in your home*' like this:

'I helped to wash and dry
3 baby vests

2 nighties
(2 to be washed later)
3 growies
2 shawls
1 bonnet
1 short frock and leggings
2 cardigans
(I only helped a bit with the christening robe).'

She showed the list to her mother.

'Would that be all the clothes a new baby would need?' she asked her.

'Yes, except for about twelve nappies.'

In the shed was her old doll's pram. She had not taken it out for ages. Today she decided to take it to the shop with her father to exchange the dog things for a baby's growy.

5 · Love from the toys

Outside the shop, Emma met Lucinda. They were both in Brownie uniform, ready for Brownies later that morning, because it was Saturday.

'What a funny old doll's pram!' said Lucinda. 'I've got a much better one than that with twin hoods and a shopping basket. I can take two of my best dolls out together,' and she looked inside Emma's. 'Whatever have you got inside yours? A nightdress case?'

'It's not,' Emma defended him. 'It's a baby boy.'

'What's his name then?' Lucinda asked.

Emma thought quickly. 'Tewksbury,' she said.

'That's not a name,' Lucinda objected, 'it's a place.'

'Tewksbury Charla-mine Albert George,' Emma insisted. 'Tewky, for short.'

'Has he been christened yet?' Lucinda asked.

'No, he's too young. He'll be christened soon.'

'Then I'll bring my best dolls to the christening in their white pram,' said Lucinda. 'Shall we have it this afternoon? Then we can tell people at Brownies this morning to bring their dolls and things?'

'All right,' Emma agreed. Then they saw Joey and Angela and told them about it.

'My pony hasn't been christened,' Joey said, 'the one I made for Toymaker's Badge. I'll bring him.'

Angela said she would bring her dolls and they would all bring their dolls' prams. They would meet in Emma's garden. She went into the shop where her father was looking at the baby clothes. He bought a primrose-coloured growy for the real baby and an orange and blue striped one for Tewksbury. Emma went home and put it on instead of the nightie. He looked more cuddly than ever.

'I'll just tuck him down in his pram,' she told her mother, 'and take him along to sleep in the fresh air outside the Brownie barn.'

That morning at Brownies everybody was very busy spring-cleaning their Six homes in the three corners of the barn. The Elves were lucky because they had a window in their corner, but of course it needed cleaning and polishing. If anybody else from another Six wanted to come and look out of this window they had to knock three times on the wall beside it and say:

> *I am one of the twelve*
> *Who isn't an Elf.*
> *Please may I peep*
> *At the cows and the sheep?'*

There were not often many cows on the Common but

sometimes Amanda's father, who was a farmer, put his sheep out to graze on the hillside. Today there were a lot of Brownies knocking on the Elves' wall because some of the sheep had lambs, and most of them were twins. They skipped about in the sunshine most gaily.

To see out of the window properly, the smaller Brownies had to keep jumping even to get just a peep.

Amanda said that one of the lambs had only been born that morning.

'But it's much more skippity than a day-old puppy,' said Jean.

'Our puppy didn't even have its eyes open for nearly two weeks. All it could do was scrabble around on its tummy squeaking,' said Jean.

'Your baby didn't have its eyes open at first either, did it?' Emma said. 'I remember seeing them all shut up. And Angela's.'

'Oh, babies have their eyes open as soon as they're born,' Sassy said, 'except when they're asleep. They're just like us.'

'Well babies and puppies can't run about when they're a day old, looking for their mothers like lambs do.'

'Lambs don't really care which are their mothers,' said Amanda. 'It's the mothers that look for their own lambs. At least they call them by bleating and if anybody else's lamb comes along they send him off.'

'Even if a lamb's own mother is ill?' Emma asked with interest.

'Even if she's dead,' Amanda said. 'Then we have to feed the lamb with a baby's bottle. We've got two at home now on bottles.'

'I'd love to give a lamb its bottle,' Emma said.

'Yes, it's nice,' Amanda agreed. 'Sometimes they suck very greedily, and sometimes they won't and you have to talk them into it. But measuring out their milk and making sure the teats of their bottles are quite clean and pure is very important too.'

'Just like a real baby,' said Emma.

The Pixies' Six home was specially good because it had a strong old beam in it that it was perfectly safe to swing on. But any Elves or Imps who wanted to swing on it had to blow three times into a crack on the wall nearby, and make a kind of whistling sound and then say:

> *'The thing about Pixies*
> *Is the way they love mixes*
> *With Sixes who are*
> *Keen to swing on their bar.'*

The taller Brownies really preferred to swing upside down with the beam held tightly under their knees. Then they would let go with their hands and lean back and touch the floor with their finger tips or if their hair was very long, like Jean's, they could sweep the floor with the ends of it.

The Pixies had extra work to do too, because their home was rather near the door, and when it was windy the leaves blew straight into their corner.

In winter everybody thought the Imps were the luckiest of all, because their Six home was not very far from the stove. For their ceremony for anyone else who wanted to come into their home, the caller had to hiss very softly three times and say:

> *'Please each kindly Imp,*
> *When we're wet and we're limp*
> *And come in from the storm,*
> *Let us come and get warm.'*

The whole Pack collected wood and carried it through the Imp home but the Imps' special job was clearing up the little bits and pieces that dropped off on their way to the stove.

Emma was an Imp and she worked away as hard as any of them making the home clean and tidy. The six upended logs of wood that they sat on had to be dusted, and the big log they used for a table had to be polished.

'Now that the spring has come,' said their Sixer, 'we could have some flowers in our vase on the table.' So Emma and Angela went off down to the stream with a mug to fill it with water. From the wood and the hedge-row on the way back they picked eight different kinds of flowers, three white, three yellow and two blue. Emma knew the yellow flowers were buttercups, cowslips and broom from the Common. Tawny said the white flowers were wood sorrel, star of Bethlehem and ladies' smock (sometimes pale pink or mauvey white, Tawny said). And the blue flowers were bugle and the cheerful little speedwell.

'The little blue speedwell flower is so small it would fit on a milk bottle top,' Angela said, 'so I think I'll draw it in my Green Brownie Pocket-book as one of the five really beautiful outdoor things.' She took her book out of her pocket and found the five circles waiting for five beautiful things.

Emma arranged the flowers in the mug and the rest of the Six looked round for any possible finishing touches.

'There's one more thing that would make it look like a home,' said Jean. 'A mummy?' 'A daddy?' 'A tele-vision?' the rest of the Six all suggested at once.

'No, we're the mothers and the fathers and when we do any acting with Brown Owl and Tawny, we're like the people on television too. All we really need,' said Jean, 'is a baby.'

'That's easy enough,' said Emma and she went out-side the barn door to where she had left Tewky in his pram and she wheeled him in. And suddenly dolls'

prams began to be wheeled in one after another and put
into all three Six homes. Lucinda's was so grand and
big that it stuck right out of her Six home and almost
into the next. It had moulded flowers on one side.

Brown Owl and Tawny came round to look at all the
homes. They were most surprised to see so many
prams.

'What are all the children doing here today?' Brown
Owl asked.

'They're all going to a christening this afternoon,'
said Lucinda. 'Emma's puppy is going to be christened.'

'Who's going to christen him?'

'Shall we ask the rector?' 'Yes, let's get him to christen the puppy.' They all started to talk at once. 'Will you ask him Tawny?' 'Please ask Monster John.'

The Brownies still called their rector Monster John because, long ago, before he married Tawny, they had mistaken him for a monster.

But before Tawny could answer, Monster John himself came in to take her home in his car.

All the Brownies started to ask Monster John if he would christen their dolls and toys. 'Please, please, Monster John.' 'I want my pony christened Firefly.' 'I want my triplets christened Delicia, Ambrosia and

Elysia.' 'And I want Tewky to be Tewksbury-some-thing-something-something-George.' 'Please, Monster John.' 'This afternoon at Emma's.' 'We'll make you some tea.'

'No,' he said. 'We don't christen toys.'

There was a moan of disappointment.

'Why not?' 'Are you too busy?' 'Then another day?'

'Why not?' Monster John repeated. 'Because christ-ening doesn't mean, as some people think it does, merely naming something. Christening – or Baptism – it's the same – is the welcoming into the church of a new member with the special washing ceremony. Water is the sign that God will clean up our lives as we believe in Jesus. You have ceremonies in Brownies, so you all know what ceremony means.'

'Oh yes.' 'Yes, we know, we have little ceremonies for asking if we can play in each other's Six homes.' 'We have a Brownie ring every week when we sing our song and salute.' 'And we have different ceremonies for giving in our pennies.' 'And most of all we have the Brownie Promise ceremony,' said Joey. 'When a new Brownie makes her Promise to do her best to do her duty to God, to serve the Queen and help other people and to keep the Brownie law.'

'A promise is made, too, in the christening ceremony,' said Monster John. 'When you were little you couldn't make the promise yourself so you had godparents to make it for you till you are old enough for them to take you to be confirmed by the Bishop. That will be when you are, say, about twelve, and old enough to make the promise yourself and understand what you are promising.'

'And a toy can't do that, because it can't understand ever,' they agreed. 'Or talk ever.' 'Nor can an animal.'

'Exactly,' said Monster John. 'And most of all nor could a toy or even an animal keep the threefold promise the godparents made for you. The promise that you will make again for yourself at your Confirmation.'

'What is the threefold promise?' asked Angela.

'First to turn your back on all horridness and beastliness, secondly – and, oh, this is a lovely one – to believe in God's love for us, and thirdly to obey the Christian law.'

'It's just like our Brownie Promise when a new Brownie is welcomed into the pack,' said Amanda. 'That's three promises in one, as well.'

'And it really means the same,' Joey said, 'doesn't it?'

'Yes, but the wonderful thing about christening is,' Monster John said, 'that God makes a promise too. He promises to answer the godparents' prayers for your soul to stay washed and clean for ever. I believe that the washing is to preserve this perfection, like washing a cut finger under the tap.'

'For just in case?' suggested Joey. 'Just in case of any

badness making the cut worse? If you've been christened and your godparents are praying for you all right, then you wouldn't want to be bad. And you'd want to stop anybody else wanting to be wicked too.'

'And toys can't be wicked anyway,' said Tulip, getting back to the point.

'So we all agree that they can't be christened?' Monster John said.

The Brownies all nodded, except Emma.

'But how can we give my Tewky a name without a ceremony?' Emma asked.

'We didn't have a ceremony when you all started calling me Monster John,' he said with another of his great big laughs.

'That's only a nickname,' Emma said.

'And Tewky's only a nickname,' said Lucinda.

'But what about his full name? Tewksbury Charlamine Albert George?' Emma just managed to remember it all this time. 'How can he get that?'

'Of course there's no reason why toys shouldn't have a naming ceremony,' said Monster John, 'like ships and bells.'

'And can we make the ceremony like a christening with some water and godfathers and godmothers?' asked Joey.

'Children have always acted weddings and funerals and christenings,' Monster John said. 'There's nothing wrong with acting a christening with godparents in it just like you act plays with kings and queens and princesses in them. Do you remember when we all acted Snow White?'

'Oh yes.' 'And Angela and Lela were both ends of the horse.' 'And Joey and Lucinda had a terrible fight because they both wanted to be Prince Charming.' 'But you were Prince Charming in the end, weren't you, Monster John?' 'And Tawny was Snow White.' 'And we were the Seven Dwarfs.'

'Except,' said Monster John, 'that we weren't *really*. We only pretended we were. And so you can pretend one of you is a parson, and pretend two are parents and pretend three are godparents and pretend your toy dog, Emma, is the baby. And God will perfectly well understand it is not a real christening.'

Monster John was just going to take Tawny home when he turned back to say, 'Although I can't christen your puppy, Emma, next Sunday, when we have had time to tell all the other children, we'll have a special toy service and you shall all bring the toys you love most, and we'll ask for God's blessing to help to make us all more loving and good and kind.'

'Like we have a special plough service to ask God to bless his work in the fields.' 'And a special harvest thanksgiving when we bring food and vegetables and corn to church to thank God for it.'

'And we'll make up a real prayer for the toy service?' Monster John asked.

'Oh yes,' said Joey, 'Jean's specially good at making
up prayers.'

At the play christening in Emma's garden that
afternoon, Lucinda decided to dress up as Monster

John and they pretended that the bird-bath was the font and that Joey and Jean were Tewksbury's godfathers and Amanda was his godmother.

'That's right. Two godfathers and one godmother for a boy,' Emma's mother said, when she came out to fill the bird-bath with water. 'And two godmothers and one godfather for a girl.'

'We'll all change round for the other animals and dolls,' said Joey. 'And I'll be Firefly's mother. Can I be Tewky's father this time?'

Emma, of course, was his mother. Over his growy Tewksbury was wearing a white frock with flowers on it borrowed from Emma's mother's baby drawer. Emma was wearing one of her grandmother's hats.

Lucinda began with the long mumble that Monster John had taught them was all right for a play christening. Then Emma held out Tewksbury and started to tell Lucinda what his names were to be. 'Tewksbury Charla-mine —'

'Charla?' Lucinda said. 'How d'you spell it?'

'C-h-a-r-l-a Charla,' Emma spelt it out. 'M-i-n-e mine.'

'Oh come on,' Lucinda said. 'That's just plain silly. I'll just call him Charlie.'

'No you won't,' said Emma, snatching him back and they both tugged so hard that somehow Tewksbury slipped out of the white frock – splash – into the water.

49

The Brownies and the christening

Emma cried. Lucinda started to stump off home with her dolls' pram, calling over her shoulder: 'I'm not having my triplets named in your silly old bird-bath.' The others got Tewksbury out of the water and tried to wring him out.

'Oh dear, he *is* wet,' said Joey. 'He'll take days to get dry.'

'It's all right,' said Emma, still sniffing a bit. 'I can take his growy off and hang it on the washing line and I can take my socks out of his tummy and hang them up too. And then he can hang up beside them. They'll soon get dry.'

The others were amazed to see how easily Tewksbury could be taken to pieces.

'Fancy having a zip! I've never seen anybody with a zip on their tummy before!' Angela said, peering at it.

'And now he's really a sort of bag,' Tulip said with interest.

'You could use him for a night-dress case,' Joey suggested.

'But I don't,' Emma said shortly.

Presently Lucinda came back and said she was sorry. After all she would like to have her triplets named Delicia, Ambrosia and Elysia, and if Emma liked, when Tewksbury was dry, she would give him any names Emma wanted, if she wrote them down first. 'And if you like,' she ended up, 'you can be Monster John when it's my triplets' turn to be done.'

Love from the toys

Two Sundays later, nearly every child in the village came to the toy service bringing a toy and some brought two. All Sassy's little brothers and sisters came dragging wooden cranes and engines and hugging rag dolls and teddy bears. Half-way through the service the children walked slowly up to the altar carrying their toys. Any who were too small to walk were carried by their mothers and fathers. The rector laid his hands on the children and blessed them and then laid his hands on the toys.

Jean had made up a special prayer and some of the Brownies had copied it out so they could all say it together.

'Oh Lord of all Heaven and Earth, please bless the love that all children all over the world have for their toys and help it make all the children kinder and more thoughtful for others. Specially bless the children who lost their own toys in the factory explosion, some even their mothers and fathers, and please help the toys that we sent them to make more love and happiness for everyone. And, dear God, please make these our toys help us all to be kinder and more helpful to each other. Amen.'

Everybody went home very happy and full of plans to make their toys help them to be more good and useful.

Even Sam said to one of his little brothers: 'Here, you can have a ride in my truck if you like,' and Lucinda said: 'Would anyone like to push my dolls' pram?'

The Brownies and the christening

Several of Sassy's and Sam's little brothers and sisters made a dash for it, but they all pushed it together, with beaming smiles and not a single harsh word.

'Jean's prayer is answered,' said Emma, wrapping Tewksbury's shawl more tightly round him.

6 · Tewky takes a bath

Emma's mother was trimming a basket with muslin for the new baby's powder and cotton wool and bathing things. She gave Emma some scraps to trim an Easter egg basket the same way with pockets round the inside and a pin-cushion for nappy pins. Emma drew a picture of it for her Brown Pocket-book, under *Brownies make things* (page 12) and made a note to ask at Brownies if she could answer *'What did you do with it?'* with 'Kept Tewky's bottle and bathing things in it.'

By now it was holiday time and there was no school. On Wednesday afternoon Emma's mother said:

'I shall have to go to the baby clinic today. Would you like to come with me or stay and play in the garden?'

'I'd like to come. But how can you go to a baby clinic when you haven't had your baby yet?'

'Oh, they have a special clinic for mothers to go to before they have their babies. We see the doctor and he makes sure our babies are safe and well inside us, and a few mothers, who have never had babies before, can learn how to look after them.'

'Then I'd certainly better come,' said Emma. 'I can manage to look after Tewksbury all right. But I don't think I'd manage very well with our new baby. I'll bring Tewky along too in case I have to wait, to give me something to do.'

They set off together with the doll's pram. As Emma's mother handed in her card at the clinic, the nurse who was in charge said:

'It's just such a pity. We were going to have a class today for the new mothers to teach them how to bath a baby, but the doll we've used for years fell off the top of the cupboard and has broken into a hundred pieces.'

Then she saw Emma's doll's pram.

'Why you've got a baby doll in your pram,' she said.

'Yes,' Emma said taking Tewky out. 'He's called Tewksbury. Well Tewksbury Charlamine Albert George, really. But please borrow him to show the new mothers how to bath a baby. Can I watch too?'

The nurse looked at him more closely.

'He looks more like a dog than a baby,' she said. 'But never mind, he fits beautifully into his real baby clothes so, if you don't mind me undressing him, he'll be fine. I shan't use real water.'

'Oh, it doesn't matter,' Emma said, 'it won't hurt him. He got soaked at his pretence christening, and we just hung him on the line to dry.'

'He wouldn't dry quickly enough here for me to dress him again after his bath,' said nurse.

Emma's mother went off to be weighed.

When all the new mothers had arrived they sat down and nurse brought out the baby bath and put it on its stand.

'Not all babies like being undressed,' nurse said, taking Tewksbury from Emma, 'but this little blessing looks so good I don't think we shall hear a sound,' and Emma remembered the toy service.

Nurse sat down on a low chair with Tewksbury, on a large bath-towel, across her knees. Beside her she had placed a real baby basket with soap and powder and cotton wool in it. Emma, sitting with the mothers, glowed with pride. Nurse started to undress Tewksbury as though he were a real baby. She gathered up each sleeve between her fingers and thumb and eased it over each paw, talking away, as she did it.

'Little fingers can get uncomfortably bent the wrong way if you let them get lost in a long tunnel of a sleeve,' she said, and chatted on about not sitting in a draught or letting him roll on to the floor. She wrapped him quickly in another towel before pretending to wash his hair. She held him over the edge of the bath and pretended to rinse it and then dry it on her knee. Then she showed how to wash each eye with a special piece of cotton wool, then his nose, then each pink ear before throwing away the cotton wool. Only when she unwrapped him to show how to soap him all over did the mothers see the zip down his front. Emma felt terrible but the mothers were mostly very kind and nobody mentioned nightdress cases.

Nurse showed them how to lift a baby into the bath with one arm under his shoulder, holding tight to the opposite leg, with the other hand steadying him as she lowered him gently into the bath. 'There he goes!' she clucked. 'Helping to splash the soap off as he kicks! And isn't he enjoying himself? He mustn't stay in for too long or he'll catch cold.'

She lifted Tewksbury out on to the towel on her lap to pat him dry with the other towel. She showed how to put a nappy on without spiking the baby with a safety-pin and when she had dressed him again she wrapped him tightly in his shawl.

'New-born babies love being wrapped up very tightly,' she said. 'And now he's ready for his next feed.'

'I know a dog,' Emma could not help whispering to the mother next to her, 'called Lady Lardy Cake who feeds her own puppies. And I also know someone who feeds lambs with bottles.'

She had been so interested in watching nurse that she had hardly noticed that another mother had come in late and was sitting at the back. Now, as Emma got up for nurse to hand Tewksbury back to her, she saw that the late-comer was Tawny. She gave her a smile and for a moment Tawny seemed quite surprised to

see a Brownie at the Mothercraft Class. Emma went over to talk to her.

'Did you see it was my Tewksbury who was used to show how to bath new babies?' Emma asked.

'Yes, I did. You must be very proud of him.'

'It wasn't anything I did specially,' Emma said, 'but he *was* blessed in church. I just came with Mummy. Are you going to have a baby too?'

Tawny smiled very slowly.

'Yes, I hope so,' she said. 'Your Mummy knows how

to look after babies because she had you. But I don't so I've had to come to learn.'

'Oh, don't worry,' Emma said, 'you can be quite sure you'll have plenty of help from the Brownies. Specially Sassy with all those little brothers and sisters.'

'Let's not tell the other Brownies about my baby yet,' said Tawny.

'Why ever not?' Emma asked. 'Aren't you and Monster John excited that you're going to have a baby?'

'Very excited,' Tawny agreed, 'but I just wanted to keep it as a great big surprise for a bit later on.'

Emma nodded understandingly.

'It could be a pow-wow surprise, you could tell us in a sort of whisper to start with,' Emma said, 'and then we could turn it into a sort of play or ceremony. But I'll keep it a secret till you say – even if I nearly burst.'

'I think there ought to be a special badge for Brownies who manage to keep a secret for a long time,' said Tawny.

As soon as Emma got home she got out her Brown Pocket-book to see how she could finish filling in the page about Brownies helping at home. There was no more room left on page sixteen, so she turned to the end of the book and found the picture of an elephant with a knot tied in his trunk, and under *Things to remember*, she pencilled in some useful ideas nurse had mentioned all ready for when she could help her mother to look after their new baby.

'What ever are these?' Brown Owl asked, when she saw them.

'I can rub them out if they aren't very good ways of helping at home,' Emma said, but Brown Owl went on looking at them with perplexed interest.

'The triangle? The oblong? The twisted? The kite?' Brown Owl read them out. 'Are they cakes or birds or musical instruments or what?'

'They really belong to the page that asks what new ways you have learnt lately to help clothes in your home,' Emma explained. 'They're different ways of folding nappies.' She was just going to say how useful they could be to the whole Pack when Tawny had had her baby, because the Brownies could go along and fold them for her in the chosen shape and leave a nice pile airing for her, when she remembered, just in time, that it was Tawny's secret.

All through Brownies, she kept remembering things Tawny had missed at the baby bathing lesson, and she longed to tell her. Once or twice she was able to give her a hint or two while nobody was near. 'Make sure the bath water isn't too hot by dipping your elbow in,' she said, and: 'Don't start sprinkling powder on your baby till you've patted him dry all over or the powder will turn into a sort of pudding.'

'Thank you,' Tawny said gratefully. 'I shall certainly remember.'

7 · Doll's house venture

Although it was hard work keeping the secret to start with, there were soon so many other things to think about it became quite easy.

For instance, there was the Doll's house venture. In the children's ward of the nearest hospital there were plenty of big toys for children to scoot or pedal on when they were dressed and well enough to play out of bed. One of Sassy's little brothers had been in hospital and had the time of his life.

'He said there was an engine and a tricycle and a racing car and a fire engine,' Sassy said. 'He didn't want to come home! But when my little sister was in hospital she was in bed a long time and when she got up she was not strong enough to romp about with the other children. There were dolls and books and older children to play table games with her but most of the games were too difficult for her. What she needed was something quiet and easy to play with.'

The Brownies put their heads together in a pow-wow and tried to think what would be a good present for the hospital that they could make themselves for children just beginning to get better.

'Scrap books.' 'Paper dolls.' 'Hand puppets.' 'Weaving.' 'Indoor gardening.' There was a babble of ideas.

Then Jean said:

'What about a doll's house? It's a nice easy gentle thing to play with if you're not feeling very strong.'

Brown Owl agreed it was a wonderful idea.

'We can make the house out of cardboard. Grocery boxes that are divided in the middle.' 'Two of those side by side would make four rooms.' 'Or two wooden orange boxes. That would make four rooms too.' 'We really only need three rooms. One for each Six to furnish.' 'One could be the hall with the stairs in it and we could all furnish that.'

But when the Brownies brought grocery boxes and orange boxes, and tried them out for size, Lucinda said:

'None of these looks very like a house. My doll's house is a classical villa with pillars and a balcony round the top.'

'Then why don't you give your classical doll's house to the hospital if it's so wonderful?' her cousin Tulip said with a cousinly nudge.

Lucinda took a very deep breath and went rather pink and everybody looked at her.

'You know,' she said, 'I believe – I think – it's just what I will do.'

'That's a very kind and generous thought Lucinda,'

Brown Owl said, 'and I'm very glad you offered. But I think we must ask your mother first whether she would like you to.'

'Oh, Lucinda's mother and father always let her do anything she wants to,' said Tulip.

'Of course they will,' Lucinda said. 'But there's only one thing. My doll's house is beautiful outside but we should have to do it up inside.'

'The walls are in a pretty bad state,' said Tulip, who knew it well, 'and most of the furniture. And some of it's lost.'

'Couldn't that be the Venture then?' said Joey. 'Repapering the walls and making new curtains and mending the furniture and adding little bits and pieces? And then we can all wear V badges to show we are on a Venture together.'

'And we can fill our Venture in on the special page in our Pocket-books,' said Angela. 'How many rooms has the doll's house got?'

'A big hall and a sitting-room and a kitchen and a bedroom with a kind of bathroom off it,' said Tulip: she had played with it almost as often as Lucinda.

'Can we do the kitchen?' said all the Elves at once. 'And us Imps do the sitting-room!' 'And us Pixies do all the upstairs?'

The next week, just before Brownies, Lucinda's father took her doll's house up to the Brownie barn in his car. He lifted it out and brought it in, and all the

Brownies gathered round. Lucinda opened the two
great doors that formed the front wall with the front
door and the windows in it, and each Six in turn took
out the furniture from their chosen room and took
them off to their Six home.

Angela's father was a builder and had given the Pack
a whole great big book of wallpapers. Each page was
just a bit bigger than each of the walls in the rooms. All
four walls in each room had to have a slightly different
pattern, but that made it all the more fun. The
Brownies decided to paper the ceiling and floors of
each room as well, so this gave every single Brownie a
chance to choose one paper and stick it on.

This led to a certain amount of disagreement. 'But
we can't have a pink ceiling and a hunting picture floor
and seagulls on one wall and roses on the other.' 'Blue

and green should not be seen.' 'Just when I've chosen such a pretty rosy pattern, Angela has to go and put a ghastly lot of green sticks beside it.' 'Couldn't we have a white ceiling and a brown floor instead of a brown ceiling and a white floor? White shows footmarks so badly.'

When Tawny had given each Six some paste and brushes, each Brownie in turn measured up her wall or floor or ceiling by putting a sheet of newspaper against it and folding the edges back to make it fit. She pressed the newspaper hard against any doors or windows or a fireplace and then drew round them with a pencil, and afterwards copied the shape of the whole on to her piece of wallpaper and cut out windows, doors and fireplaces. Luckily there was so much wallpaper in the book that if anything went wrong there was enough to start again in a slightly different colour.

When all the rooms had been papered the Brownies decided to finish the rooms off with skirting-boards at the bottom (cut from strips of plain wallpaper) and friezes at the top (cut from borders in the pattern book). In the wallpaper book there was some stiff paper made to look like wood, and the Brownies used this for making doors, window frames and to cover the floor of the hall. The Pixies papered the bathroom wall and floor with paper that looked like tiles.

The following week everybody brought needles and cotton and little scraps of material for making new curtains and re-covering the furniture. Each Six worked in its own Six home. Some of Lucinda's furniture was so broken it was not worth mending.

Here are some of the ideas Brownies got from their mothers or grandmothers or invented themselves for making new furniture. *Chairs* made by threading small beads on strong wire and bending it into the shape of chair-back and legs, then filling in the seat with cardboard with velvet stuck on it, fixed on with ends of the wire specially left over for the job. *Beds* made out of small cardboard boxes with curtains made for them, and cots made of match-boxes. *Tables* from cork, pins and wool. (Stick the pins in all round the cork and weave the wool in and out). Chair backs and legs made from pins with wool woven in between. *A clothes basket* made the same way. *A baby's cradle* out of half a walnut shell lined, with curtains hanging from a match-stick wedged upright into one end of the shell. *A chest of drawers* from three pairs of match-boxes stuck together, with gold bend-back paper-clips for drawer handles. *Table lamps* from beads threaded tightly on to stiff wire, with paper shades. They made table-cloths and mats and a tiny *roller-towel* for the kitchen. Everything had to be made of the thinnest and finest material so that it did not look bulky. They made *screens* out of postcards, *flowerpots* out of corks covered in red paper and *flowers* out of coloured tissue-paper and fuse wire. Amanda even made some tiny *knitting* by casting thick cotton

65

on to two large pins and knitting two rows and then rolling the rest of the cotton up into a tiny ball. She gummed it here and there so that it would not become unravelled.

On a wet windy day when it was cold enough to need the stove, Brown Owl brought some plain flour and salt and a little water and the Brownies helped her mix it into a stiff paste, like clay. They moulded it into the shapes of a round of beef, a chicken, a leg of mutton, potatoes, cauliflower, carrots, pies, bananas, oranges, apples and cakes. Amanda made a birthday cake and stuck tiny bits of match-sticks in for candles.

Then they started to make other things. The Elves made a tiny tea-set, squashing out the little cups and jugs and a tea-pot by pushing a pencil into a very small ball of dough and then taking it out and pinching handles in it. The Imps made ornaments and a clock for the sitting-room and the Pixies made candlesticks and tooth mugs for upstairs.

When they were done they put them on flat tin lids very near to the stove so that they would dry off slowly and become quite hard by the next week when anybody who had a paint box brought it.

First everything was painted white from the tubes of white paint that some of their paint boxes had in them. Once this had dried the Brownies painted patterns on the things that were meant to be china and they painted the food to look like real food. The tea-set had a little

tiny rosy border and the rims of the cups were picked
out in pink. For the kitchen, the roast beef was painted
in rounds of red, leaving white streaks for the fat. The
apples were green on one side and rosy on the other.
The bananas had blackish-grey streaks on their yellow
sides. Amanda painted Happy Birthday on her tiny
birthday cake, and she cut a strip of paper into a minia-
ture frill and stuck it on round it.

The kitchen Brownies cut out rounds of cardboard
for dishes and stuck their food on to them.

They made goblets from silver paper and saucepans
from screwtop lids with wire handles.

'What about the people?' Angela suddenly asked.
'We may be the mothers and fathers and children in our
own Six homes, but a sick child in hospital would need
some people to play with in the doll's house.'

So the next thing to make was a mother, a father, two
children, a baby and a dog. Brown Owl brought some
pipe cleaners and wool and wire and out came the
needles and cotton and scissors again.

When the doll's house was finished Brown Owl was
so pleased with it she asked Tawny to bring Monster
John to see it. *He* was so pleased with it he said how nice
it would be to have it in the church for a little while for
everybody to see before it went to the hospital.

'And will you ask for a blessing for it like at our toy
service?' Emma asked. 'So it makes the ill children who
play with it happy?'

67

And so Lucinda's father took it down to the church in his car and the Brownies met it there again with Monster John, who put his hand on the top chimney and said: 'God bless this house, made lovely and fresh again by many loving little hands. God bless the children who play with it and may the happiness in remaking it go on to them as they play. God bless the child who gave her doll's house to give so much happiness.'

All the Brownies said 'Amen' and then they sang the song, 'God Bless this House'.

Amanda had written out a notice to put by the doll's house saying that the Brownies restored this house for the children's ward of the hospital. They left the doors open for everyone to see inside.

Nobody would have guessed that the first child to play with it in hospital would be one of themselves.

8 · Do I have to?

At the next Brownie pow-wow Brown Owl said:

'Has anyone any secrets to tell?'

Emma looked at Tawny and Tawny looked at Emma and nodded.

'Yes,' said Tawny. 'I've got a secret to tell but I am going to let Emma tell it for me because it's been her secret too and she's kept it so well for so long. Go on Emma, you tell.'

Emma whispered Tawny's secret so softly that at first nobody heard.

'Go on, Emma.' 'Louder.' 'We can't hear, say it again.'

Emma said it again but still nobody heard.

The third time everybody heard.

'Tawny's going to have a darling little Brownie baby.'

'Tawny?' 'A baby?' 'A baby for our own Pack!' 'Please let us look after it!' 'Can't it be our next Venture?'

'This will be Tawny's own Venture!' Brown Owl said with a smile.

'And Monster John's,' added Sassy.

'But we can make it little clothes.' 'We can knit it vests.' 'We can make it little bonnets.' 'And when it arrives we can push it about in its pram.'

'Then I should like it to be a Brownie Venture,' said Tawny.

So Tawny's baby became the Pack's next Venture and everybody was given a V badge to pin on to her uniform while they all helped to get ready for the baby. This time the Venture was not divided up into Sixes as with the doll's house but the whole Pack took part together. The Brownies who could knit made vests and jerseys and a bonnet. And Emma and two other Brownies trimmed a baby basket just like the one Emma's mother had trimmed for her baby.

Each knitter made a square and all these different coloured squares were sewn together to make a pram cover.

Now all the Brownie talk was about baby clothes and baskets and carry-cots. Emma decided it was time Tewksbury grew a bit. His growy still sagged in one or two places so she stuffed them out with more of her socks and the growy stretched nicely over them. The result was that next Monday morning, Emma was nearly late for school because her mother could not find a pair of clean socks.

'I can't think what's happened to them,' her mother said. 'There have always been enough before.'

'Socks?' Emma said. 'Oh, that's all right. Don't you remember? They're inside Tewky.' And she un-popped Tewksbury's growy and unzipped his tummy and took a pair of clean socks out and put them on. Her mother came in as she was doing him up again.

'Now he's got all thin again,' she said. 'I shall have to find something else to stuff him with.'

And when Emma came home from school there was Tewksbury looking plumper than ever and there were all her socks in a neat row in her drawer.

'He's got some strips of an old very darned blanket inside him,' her mother said, 'and there's still some left if you want him to grow any more later. But he's already much bigger than my new baby will be when it's born.'

They sat down to tea.

'Isn't it time we had our new baby?' Emma said. 'The summer's here and it seems ages and ages since I wanted a puppy.'

'It won't be long now,' her mother said. 'We can't tell exactly which day but perhaps in about a week. As I've got rather fat and feel a bit tired Daddy and I thought it would be a good idea for you to go for a little seaside holiday at Cobble to two old aunts of Daddy's who have asked you to stay.'

'But if you're tired, Mummy,' Emma said, 'you'll need me here to help you.'

The Brownies and the christening

'You'll enjoy being at Cobble-by-the-Sea,' her mother said, 'it's a lovely place and you can write to me and I'll write to you. We've never done that yet.'

'We can easily do that without me going away,' Emma said.

After tea she proved it by going up to her room and writing a letter to her mother, putting it in an envelope and sticking it up and putting it on the kitchen table.

She went out into the garden because there was no point in writing a letter if she was there to see and hear it read.

Her mother found it just as her father came in from work. She opened it and read it out:

'Dear Mummy,
Please do not let me go away to stay with Daddy's
old aunts. I need to stay and Lend a Hand because
you are getting fat and tired. I must be here too to
help with our new baby. Love and kisses and hugs,
Emma.'
XXX

It ended up with a picture of their new baby.

'Of course she'll love it when she gets there,' said her father. 'I used to stay with them when I was a little boy and it was great fun on the beach. They were a bit strict with me,' he said, 'but then I was a boy and Emma is much better behaved than I was. She'll be a help to them too as she's a Brownie.'

'I wonder if she ought to go,' her mother said. 'It's quite true, she is a great help here. She saves me running up and down the stairs.'

'We've told the aunts she's coming,' said her father, 'they'll have got all ready for her.'

He called Emma in from the garden and told her all about the fun he had had with the fishermen and in the market place at Cobble when he was her age.

'But I don't like fishing,' Emma said, 'or market places. I want to stay here and do the washing-up for Mummy.'

'But you can do the washing-up for the aunts,' her father said. 'They're both quite old now and really need a bit of help.'

'Yes,' said her mother, 'they really need help more than I do. You see I have you all the time and for them it will be a special treat. Of course you'll take Tewky and all his things with you, won't you?'

'Oh yes, I couldn't go without Tewky,' Emma picked him up from his cot with her hand under his head as she had seen nurse doing at the clinic, and gently turned him over before she gave him a gentle hug.

'Shall I lend you my own little writing-case to pack his things in?' her mother asked.

'Oh, yes please,' said Emma, 'and I can pack my own

things. It's one of the things we learn to do on the Brownie footpath.'

Soon Emma was so interested in packing and getting ready to go to the seaside that she forgot she had wanted to stay at home. She put her own shoes and heavy things in the bottom of the suitcase her mother gave her and then came her underclothes, jeans and sweaters; round the sides she fitted the knobbly things like her brush and comb bag and her sponge bag and in the corners she fitted the socks that had been inside Tewksbury. She folded her dresses carefully on her bed and put them on the top.

'I'll take my Brownie uniform,' she said, 'to wear in church on Sundays.'

Then she packed Tewksbury's things in her mother's little writing-case. 'There's only one thing,' she said to her mother as they said goodbye, when she was all ready for her father to take her to Cobble. 'If I don't get back in time for our new baby, you will tell me at once if it's a boy or a girl.'

'Of course, darling,' her mother kissed her. 'Daddy will make sure that you are the first to know.'

9 · Don't, don't, don't!

Emma sat by the window of the front room of the great aunts' house at Cobble. Behind the lace curtains the rain streamed down the window panes and hid the cold grey misty sea. She had never felt so miserable in her life. But for Tewksbury, whom she had hardly put down in his cot for a moment since she arrived, she would already have been crying. When she got into bed she was going to cry as much as she liked. She had tried the Brownie smile and it helped a bit but Aunt Aurora, the elder of the two very old aunts, had told her not to make silly faces, so the smile had gone and with it the hope that things would soon be better.

As for trying the Brownie dodge of humming a little tune to cheer yourself up, the aunts had just said, 'Must you make that annoying noise?' and when Emma had tried to take her mind off not being at home by practising some of the things she wanted to fill in her Brown Pocket-book in the last page but one, the aunts just said, 'Do stop being so silly.'

She had sat on the floor cross-legged and got up without using her hands a few times, she had said the alphabet backwards, but under her breath. She had stood quite still listening to the birds and tried to recognise their songs over and above the gulls. She had sat at the bottom of the garden with a pencil and looked along the line of houses and all the different television aerials and then sketched them on the blank page at the end of her brown book.

'What ugly things to draw,' said Aunt Clarice. 'Why don't you draw the sea?' Emma did not say the sea looked too ugly and boring even to look at let alone draw. Aunt Aurora came in while she was dressing. Emma could now not only dress herself completely with her eyes shut all the time, but she could fold up the tops and the bottoms of her pyjamas, and she could wash her face, neck and hands, clean her teeth, and brush her hair and put away all her washing and brushing things without opening her eyes from start to finish.

'What a silly thing to do,' said Aunt Clarice when she saw her crossing the room arms out to feel for things and eyes tightly shut. 'Open your eyes at once. You'll trip over something. How can you expect to put your clothes on straight if you don't look what you're doing?'

'Blind people have to,' Emma said. 'I want to know how difficult it is for them.'

It was don't, don't, don't all the time.

The last straw was when Emma put a piece of tissue-paper over her comb and blew the tune of 'God Save the Queen' on it. She was just starting off on the Brownie song when Aunt Aurora burst in with her hands over her ears.

But the hardest thing of all to bear was the aunts refusing to let Emma help them in any way and laughing at her when she did the kind of things she was used to doing naturally at home without asking if she could help.

'Don't pick up the plates, you might drop them.' 'Don't go to the door when anyone knocks, it won't be for you.' 'Don't bring in the milk, it's too heavy.' 'Don't bring in the letters, you'll only make them grubby.'

When she had offered to make sandwiches for tea, they both almost screamed, they were so shocked. 'Sandwiches? A child of your age with a knife? What an idea,' said Aunt Aurora.

'And very funny sandwiches they'd be, I should think,' said Aunt Clarice.

And now on her second day Emma was looking out of the window longing and longing to go home. If her mother knew how beastly it was she would send for her at once. That was what decided her to write to her mother. There were pieces of paper with the name of the house printed on them, *The Gables, Cobble,* on a writing desk and Emma took a sheet and started off with her pencil.

The Brownies and the christening

'*Dear Mummy,*
Please let me come home. The aunts don't like me
here. I am in their way and they can't get on. I
should be much more use at home. I could help to
get ready for the new baby. If I don't come home
soon I shall miss two weeks of Brownies.
>   *Love, Emma.*
>   *XXX*

She read it through and then thought how sad it
would make her mother, so with the india rubber on the
end of her pencil she rubbed out 'Mummy' and put
'Sassy' instead and she rubbed out 'please let me'
and put in 'I want to'. She put it in one of the envelopes
on the writing desk and stuck it up, knowing it could do
no good but it made her feel better that a friend knew
how miserable she was. The envelope was the kind that
had a stamp printed into it so she put the right number
of pennies out of her purse into the envelope rack to
pay for it, and then went out to the post-box at the end of
the street. On the way back she met Aunt Aurora, with
her umbrella still up although the rain had nearly
stopped. 'What are you doing out here in the street
alone?' she asked.

Emma did not want to tell a lie so she was just going
to say she had been to the post when Aunt Clarice came
out and they both had a quarrel over whether or not
Emma should be in the street by herself. Her father had

gone out by himself at her age. But he was a boy. They were so cross with each other they had forgotten all about Emma.

When the postman came Emma could see there was a letter for her in her mother's handwriting. The aunts could hardly complain that she had made her own letter grubby, but as she opened it they came in.

'What are you doing opening our letters?' said Aunt Aurora.

'It's a letter for me,' said Emma, 'from mummy.'

'Shall I read it to you then?' said Aunt Clarice.

But Emma hung on to it tight. 'No, thank you, I can read it myself.'

'Then read it out so we can hear how well you read.'

Emma felt like reading out something quite different from what her mother had written because it was all good and lovely and made her feel happy again. She felt like making up rubbish about how she had made herself a new hat, although her mother never wore hats. But the aunts stood so near to her they made her read what was written:

'*Darling Emma,*' she said.
'*Daddy and I miss you so much. You are always such a help. I hope Tewksbury is enjoying the seaside and taking his food like a good baby. Everything is ready now for our other baby and if you help to look after it as well as you do Tewksbury, and love it*

79

half as much, we shall all be very lucky. Give our
love to Aunt Aurora and Aunt Clarice, with heaps of
kisses from Mummy.

XXX

Emma could see from the great aunts' faces they were
thinking '*how silly*'. One said, 'Fancy writing in a letter
about a doll.' And the other said, 'I suppose she's
writing about another baby doll?'

'Oh no,' said Emma, 'she's writing about her own
baby. Didn't Daddy tell you she's having a new baby
quite soon?'

'*We* knew this,' said Aunt Aurora. 'But we hardly
expected that you would be told.'

'But it's going to be our baby,' said Emma. 'It's
never been a secret for me.' She was thinking of
Tawny's baby and the secret she had kept so long. She
took her letter to her room so she could read it all by
herself again and again. She was so afraid the aunts
might take it away from her that she unpopped
Tewksbury's growy and unzipped his tummy and hid
the letter safely inside him. Then she did him up again
and tucked him down to sleep. Emma thought of all the
nice things she could say to her mother when she wrote
back. She was glad now she had not sent her the letter
she had posted to Sassy. Aunt Aurora called her down.

'There you are, Emma,' she said, sitting her down at
the table. 'I've written out a letter for you to copy to

your mother. Take great care to write neatly and remember to put in the commas.'

'But I can write my own letter,' Emma said. 'We have to write letters for our Hostess Badge in Brownies and we never copy them.'

'Come along, child,' said the aunt. 'Do as you are told.' So Emma had to copy out:

> *'Dear Mother,*
> *It is very pleasant here with my two great-aunts,*
> *who are doing so much to make the visit a success.*
> *The weather has not yet been favourable for the*
> *beach but they hope to take me there when it clears.*
> *Hoping this finds you, as it leaves me, in good*
> *spirits, Your affectionate daughter, Emma.'*

Well anyway, thought Emma, Mummy would know perfectly well she had not thought it up herself, so she copied it out and put in the commas.

Next day, although the weather cleared, there was no talk of going to the beach. Emma went down to the bottom of the garden with Tewksbury and leant on the wall to watch the people going down to the beach. The children carried bathing towels, buckets and spades, and shrimping nets, and the parents carried picnic baskets and rugs to lie on. An old fisherman came up the gangway with a basket full of live crabs wriggling about with their claws waving.

There was a tree on the other side of the pathway

and Emma stayed quite still while she listened to the bird singing on it to see if she could recognise its song. There was something about it she had heard before and yet it seemed a very long song for any ordinary bird. It kept on repeating the same tune again and again and then more and more clearly she realised the tune had real words. Not just the, 'a little bit of bread and no cheese,' that Tawny said Yellow-Hammers said. These really were words and they seemed to be, 'If you're fed up here and want to go home I'll take you. If you're fed up here and want to go home I'll take you. If you're fed up here and want to go home I'll take you.' It was very odd and Emma began to think she must be just *wanting* the bird to sing this song. Or better still, she was in a kind of fairy story. She peered across into the tree and then she saw what kind of a bird it was. It was not a bird at all, it was a boy. And it was not an ordinary boy either, it was Sassy's twin brother, Sam.

'Oh Sam,' she almost whispered across the gangway. 'How did you know I was here? How did you know I hate it here?'

'You sent your address to sister Sassy,' Sam sang back like a bird. 'You sent your address to sister Sassy. You sent your address to sister Sassy.'

If the great-aunts had heard, they would never have guessed it was not a bird song.

'So Sassy has got my letter already and sent you along to rescue me?' Emma said excitedly.

'Not really rescue,' said Sam. 'I just came on my own to take you home.'

'I couldn't really go without saying goodbye to the great-aunts and thanking them for having me,' Emma said. 'And then they'd make me stay.'

Sam did not come down the tree in the ordinary way. He seemed to be flying like a bird. Then quite suddenly, to Emma's amazement, she saw that he had swung across the gangway on a rope attached to a higher branch. He landed beside her and let the rope swing back.

'Then just say goodbye to them and cut and run,' advised Sam. 'I'll be here to help you.'

Emma shook her head. 'It would upset my mother too much,' she said. 'That's why I didn't write and tell her how beastly it is here.'

'It upset Sassy all right, you writing to her,' said Sam. 'That's why I came.'

'Thank you,' said Emma. She never would have guessed how pleased she could be to see Sam the terrible.

'I'm sorry I worried Sassy but I am glad you came,' Emma said. 'Tell her not to worry. They don't actually smack me or hit me, just don't, don't, don't all the time, and they won't let me help them.'

'I'd rather be smacked,' said Sam. He started to climb back over the wall. 'There's a very good climbing play-ground down there near the beach,' he said. 'Will you come?'

'They wouldn't let me.'

'Oh well, if you change your mind that's where I'll be and I'll be there tomorrow too.'

'How did you get here, Sam?' Emma asked.

'On my bike. It's only seven miles each way.' He shinned up the tree and loosened the rope and brought it down with him. 'Oh, by the way, I had a look at your mum this morning. She's all right.'

'Did you tell her you were coming?'

'Oh no, she didn't see me. I just saw her. Cheerio.' And he was gone.

On Sunday Emma dressed in her Brownie uniform for church. The aunts started to say it was silly almost before she sat down to breakfast.

'Haven't you brought a proper Sunday frock?' one asked. 'You can't go to church with all those stupid little pictures sewn all over your arms. The whole idea's quite silly. It's much too much like soldiers.'

'There's nothing silly about Brownies,' Emma said, 'and nothing silly about soldiers. But Brownies aren't meant to be soldiers. We're people who promise to be good and help other people – specially the Queen and specially at home.'

The aunts could hardly say this was silly so they told her the cross-over tie was crooked and that she ought to have more salt with her egg.

She did not tell them that their hats were crooked or their dresses dowdy as they set off for church. Just as they were going in she saw something wonderful, something that at the back of her mind she had hoped would be there. It was the Cobble Brownie Pack collecting round their Brownie Guider, all in Brownie uniform like her own, and all jumping about and chattering just like her own Pack at home. How she longed to be with the Cobble Pack instead of with her two stiff great-aunts. But at any rate she could see that some of the Brownies had spotted her uniform and noticed her.

As they all came out at the end of the service their Brown Owl came up to her and gave a friendly salute and asked which Pack she belonged to.

Emma was glad it was the Brownie Guider and not one of the Brownies because she knew the great-aunts would have pulled her away. Instead they started to tell the Brownie Guider that she was staying with them and was their great-niece.

'We're having Brownie sports on the beach to-morrow,' said the Brownie Guider. 'Wouldn't your great-niece like to come and join in?'

The aunts took quite a long time to agree, and then only if it were fine and Emma was not too shy to go.

'I'd love to go to Brownie sports,' Emma said. 'I'm not a bit shy.'

'Thirza says we must all bring teddy bears or some sort of furry toy like that for an obstacle race,' one of the Brownies told Emma.

'Thirza?' Emma looked puzzled.

'Yes, that's what we call our Brownie Guider.'

'We call ours Brown Owl,' Emma said. 'And we call our Assistant Brownie Guider Tawny.'

'We used to call ours Brown Owl and Tawny once,' said another Brownie, 'but when they left we chose new names. Thirza says that's a good one for a Brownie Guider because it means acceptance and she has to accept so much with a smile.'

'And Nora means ninth. She's the ninth Assistant Brownie Guider this Pack has had,' said another Brownie, 'so we christened her that.'

'We've had the same Brown Owl and the same Tawny ever since anyone in the Pack can remember,' said Emma. 'Even after we got our Tawny married to our rector, we still go on calling her Tawny. And we call our rector Monster John.'

'What a lovely name!'

They all laughed when Emma told them how they had mistaken him for a monster when he first camped on their Common. Emma thought of telling them how he had explained that giving someone a name was not the same as christening her and so they could not really have christened their Tawny, Nora. But she thought she had better wait till she knew them better.

'I suppose you have brought a teddy with you or something like that?' said the first Brownie to talk to Emma.

Emma was just going to say, 'I've got a baby,' when

87

she remembered that Tewksbury was also a puppy. So she said, 'Oh, yes, that's all right, I've got a sort of toy dog.'

For an obstacle race he had better grow up very quickly and stop being a baby and be a dog. Emma decided to take off his baby clothes, until she remembered his zip and how he might be accused of being a nightdress case. He looked very cuddly in his growy, even as a dog, so she took off his vest and nappy, and put him down on the floor beside her so that she could get used to the idea of seeing him on all fours. She could hardly wait for Monday, and the aunts could see her excitement and started telling her if she didn't do this and didn't do that they would have to think of a punishment for her, and she knew very well what punishment they had in mind. She was so afraid of doing the wrong thing that she asked to go to bed early to get herself safely out of the way from doing anything punishable.

'Aren't you feeling well then?' Aunt Aurora said. 'Have you got a pain? Have you caught a chill?'

'I don't think she ought to go out tomorrow,' said Aunt Clarice. 'It might make her worse.'

'I'm very well indeed,' Emma said.

10 · Dial 999

Somehow Emma managed to get through the next morning and through two whole meals without more than a constant shower of, 'don't, don't, don'ts'. It was lovely to get back into her Brownie uniform again after lunch and to pick up Tewksbury and go down to wait for Thirza who was going to fetch her on the way to sports.

'You're not taking that silly toy,' said Aunt Aurora. 'It's time you grew out of that kind of thing.'

'They asked me to bring a toy,' Emma said. 'It's for an obstacle race.'

'Ridiculous! Why can't they use bean bags?'

But when Thirza came the aunts were quite nice and said they were going to a meeting so there was no need to bring Emma back early.

On the beach the Brownies were all waiting with their teddy bears and furry animals to start the first race. Their Brown Owl explained that all the animals were to be piled up together with the Brownies' shoes. The Brownies were to start by crossing a very difficult belt

of stones and flints in bare feet and then run across the
soft sand to their animals. Each Brownie then had to
pick out her own animal as well as her own shoes and
put them on and run to the high breakwater and climb
over it, still with her own animal. They then had to

make a new pile of animals and shoes on the other side and run to Nora and Thirza and Pack Leader who would blindfold them, then they had to run back to the pile and this time take out their own animal and shoes without being able to see them. They then had to grope their way across some more stones, only this time they had their shoes on, to the winning post.

It was a wonderful race and Emma got off to a good start because she often played about in bare feet and knew how to curl her feet round the stones instead of trying to walk flatly on them. There was no mistaking Tewksbury's pink ears and orange and blue striped growy so she soon picked him out. Her shoes were more difficult because so many of the Brownies wore the same kind of sandals. But she got them in the end and made up for lost time running on the flat sand and climbing with Tewksbury over the breakwater. Then there was the run to make the new pile of animals and shoes and Emma lost a bit of ground after she was blindfolded. She thought she started running towards the pile but found she was splashing towards the edge of the sea. So were some of the other Brownies, and she could hear their giggles and squeaks, so she turned inland and dropped down on her knees to crawl towards the place where she thought the pile of animals was. By this time several people had gathered round to watch the race and she could hear them laughing and calling to the Brownies to go this way or that way. Soon

she could hear from the squeaks of relief that some of
the Brownies had already found the pile and she made
straight for them. But all the soft toys seemed to feel
the same. Most of them had soft and floppy ears but
suddenly she remembered Tewksbury's zip fastener
and she wasted no more time feeling ears and noses and
paws and went straight for tummies. Three of the
animals were quite smooth but the next had an unmis-
takable zip down the middle. She could feel the poppers,
too, of Tewksbury's growy and she jumped up and
rushed off to where Thirza was calling like a seagull to
show where Home was.

'You've won!' she cried. 'The borrowed Brownie's
won.'

Emma pulled off her blindfold and it was true, she
had won – just. Two other Brownies were groping
their way towards Thirza just behind with their teddies;
others were still scrabbling around among the heap of
toys. The prize was a little china jug with a picture of
Cobble on one side and Thirza gave it to her at once.

Emma was not so good in the other races but that
did not matter. It was so lovely to have won a race with
Tewksbury. In fact Tewky had really won it for her.
She was not so good at long jump or high jump or
ordinary straight fast races. The Brownies were all so
friendly and nice to her it would not have mattered if she
had been last in all the sports. When it was all over
Thirza said:

'Does anyone want to go on the swings?' Several of the Brownies said 'Yes' and Emma went off with them to the 'Playdrome' which had all kinds of swings and ropes and slides and climbing towers. Thirza and Nora went with them because there was a notice outside, which Sam could not have read, saying children were not allowed to play here without an adult in charge of them. Emma was hardly surprised to find Sam at the top of the playboat mast which he had reached by the scrambling net.

The Brownies put their animals down together and went up the climbing frames and down the slides and swung on the trapezes and had a wonderful time. When all the Brownies had tried everything Thirza said it was time to go home.

'Nora is coming with me in my car,' Thirza said to the Pack Leader. 'Packy, as you go past, will you drop Emma, the visiting Brownie, at her great-aunts' house just along the gangway? It's so near she's hardly likely to get lost, but I said we would see her home so will you ring the bell and hand her over?'

Brown Owl called to them to come down and Emma, at the top of the mast, was last, and when she went to collect Tewksbury, he was nowhere to be seen. She called to the Brownies in front of her and they came back and said he was not there when they took their animals. Then Emma remembered Sam and his pranks. It would be just like him to pounce down and hide Tewksbury to tease her. She saw Sam was waiting near the exit to the playground but without Tewksbury.

Emma went straight up to him. 'Where's my Tewky?' she asked. 'What have you done with him?'

'He's probably gone off for a swing,' Sam said cheekily, 'or maybe he's gone fishing.'

'Tell me, Sam, quickly, where is he? I've got to go back with the Pack Leader to the great-aunts. You must give him back quickly.'

'I haven't got him,' Sam said. 'I don't know where he is.'

'Oh Sam, please, please,' Emma said. 'I put him down there with the other animals and now he's gone.'

'I don't know where he is,' said Sam. 'How are you getting on? Are the great-aunts smacking you yet?'

'I'm all right, it's just I must find Tewky. Pack Leader's waiting for me to take me back to the great-aunts.'

'You'd better go then.'

'How can I without Tewksbury?' She supposed Sam saying, 'Tewky might have gone for a swing', meant he had carried him up to the top of the playship mast. Emma started to climb furiously up the scrambling net.

The Brownies had all left the playground with Packy who was now calling to Emma to hurry up.

'You can't go up that way,' Sam called after her. 'You have to take it slowly and keep your hands and feet farther apart.' Emma took no notice and climbed on but suddenly she knew what he meant. Too late!

Her foot slipped and so did both hands. She felt herself falling, and then crash. She was on the ground, at first too winded to yell. But already Sam was yelling for her.

'Hi! Help! Come quick! There's been an accident!'

Thirza and Nora had already left and so had most of the Brownies when Sam began to shout. Packy came racing back along the promenade. Two fishermen, a lifeboatman, a lifeguard and several passers-by were also heading for the playground. Sam was at the emergency telephone beside the lifeboat house dialling nine-nine-nine and calling for an ambulance.

Emma had no time to pick herself up before she found herself surrounded by people all asking her to lie quite still, not to worry and everything would be all right. Except for a sore back where she had fallen and what felt like a slightly twisted ankle, once she had got her breath again she really was all right. She expected to see a few bruises in the morning but there was not enough to cry about and a Brownie smile and a bit of a hum soon cheered her up enough to put up with that discomfort.

'Poor thing, she doesn't know where she is.' 'She sounds almost as if she were singing.' 'Groaning more likely.' 'Poor thing, she must be bad.' 'Lie still, my dear, till the ambulance comes.' So Emma lay still and presently the crowd round her parted to make way for two ambulance men with a stretcher.

'Quite right not to move her,' one of the ambulance men said to the crowd all round her. 'It's best to leave it to us so we can lift her properly and do no further damage.' One of them felt her all over and only when he touched her foot did she give a little 'ow'. The other one then bandaged her feet and legs together and they lifted her gently on to the stretcher and carried her off to the ambulance which had been driven down to the promenade. Only as the stretcher was being slid into the ambulance did Emma remember that Tewksbury was still missing. She could just see that Sam was one of the people watching her being put into the ambulance and she called out to him: '*Now* will you bring me back my Tewksbury?'

The ambulance set off for the hospital with Sam on his bicycle following not far behind it.

Emma was taken into the hospital at Cobble and looked at by a nurse, a doctor, two more nurses, another doctor and an X-ray attendant. Her foot was unbandaged, bandaged up again, and then unbandaged. She was moved from the stretcher to a trolley, to a couch, to a wheel-chair, to another couch, back to a trolley, on to the X-ray table, and back into another wheel-chair, and then on to a couch again. Different nurses and porters pushed her about wherever she went. Sam tried to get in once or twice but was shooed out. If he had been carrying Tewky she would have asked to be allowed to see him, but he was not.

'The one thing that worries me,' Emma said to Packy, 'is that my great-aunts will be so cross if I'm late home.'

'Shall I go and tell them what's happened?' Packy asked.

'Well yes,' Emma said. 'Only don't let them come here. They'll only be so rude to me.'

While Packy was away a nurse wheeled Emma into the Children's Ward.

'It may be rather a long wait until the doctor sees your X-rays,' the nurse said. 'There are no other children in the Children's Ward at the moment but we have just received a wonderful present. You might like to look at it while you're waiting.' And there, right in front of Emma, was the doll's house that her own Brownie Pack had done up for the Children's Ward!

Nurse opened it up and wheeled Emma close to it. 'Isn't it a fine house? And aren't you a lucky girl to be the first person to see inside?' She hurried off before Emma had time to explain that she had already seen inside, and she had made the curtains and the baby's cradle. It was wonderful to see and pick up all the things that the Pack had so lovingly made. It was almost like being back with them all again. She took each thing out and examined it, then put it carefully back.

Packy came back with the news that the great-aunts

must still be out as she had knocked and rung and nobody came. Emma told Pack Leader all about how her own Pack had done up the doll's house and what a joy it was to see it again.

'Our Brownies would like to do something like that,' Packy said. 'Maybe we could do one for the Grange. That's a children's home near here.'

Emma was showing Packy round the doll's house when a nurse brought another patient in and put her into the bed near the window. The nurse said the child's name was Alice and warned them not to give her anything to eat as she had kept everyone awake half the night with a bad tummy-ache. She was younger than Emma and moaning quietly to herself, and at once Emma noticed that she was hugging a toy that, like the doll's house, she had seen before.

'Cheer up, Alice,' Packy said, going over to her. 'I expect your mummy will be here soon.'

The little girl shook her head and Emma tried to sign to Packy. For the doll in Alice's arms was the very one she had sent to the explosion children who had lost nearly everything, some even their mothers or fathers. It was easy to recognise her old doll's over-washed face, the floppy eyes and the green pattern on the dress that Emma's mother had made out of scrap left over from one of her own dresses.

'I didn't keep *every*one awake,' Alice said. 'There's twenty children at the Grange. I only woke a few.'

'The Grange?' Packy repeated. 'We were just talking about the Grange as you came in.'

'That's where I went to live after our home was blown up in a factory explosion,' the little girl said. 'And my mum.'

'Anyway your baby doll is fast asleep,' Emma said. 'What's her name?'

'Dolly,' said the little girl. 'She's my own baby doll and I love her best.' She kissed its pale shrunken face, and Emma was so glad that Alice had a toy to hug, specially if she had no mother, that she forgot that she herself, just at that moment, had neither.

A nurse came in and wheeled Emma off to the doctor, telling Pack Leader to come too. Emma knew Packy was only sixteen, but when the doctor saw her he said:

'Sit down, Mother. I'm glad to say we have X-rayed your little girl and find that she has had a lucky escape. There was no damage done and so you can take her home and give her a good tea.'

'Won't she have to stay in the hospital then?' Packy asked.

'No, she's quite all right. I think if she had cried a bit when she fell off the swing nobody would have worried, but I see from her uniform she's a Brownie, and so, of course, she was extra brave.' He gave her a smile and Emma who was holding her shoes, put them on and climbed off the wheel-chair and she and Packy almost ran out of the hospital together.

The Brownies and the christening

'It was all Sam's fault,' Emma said. 'If he hadn't shouted so loudly and made everybody come, and sent for an ambulance, I should be back at the great-aunts by now.'

'Was it Sam's fault that you didn't come when I called you?' Packy asked. And Emma knew whose fault it was. Not Sam's but her own.

'Never mind, as the great-aunts weren't in, you would have had to wait on the doorstep anyway,' Packy said.

'And at least now we know what it's like inside the hospital,' Emma said, 'and I loved seeing our doll's house again. I'd have liked to stay in the Children's Ward for a bit. It's much more fun than with my great-aunts.'

Now when they rang the bell, the door was opened and great-aunt Aurora came out. She thanked Packy for bringing Emma.

'You're back earlier than we expected,' she said. 'No doubt you have had your tea,' and before Emma had time to say she had not and was very hungry and thirsty Aunt Aurora said, 'I've written another letter for you to copy to your mother,' and she put her down at the table in front of it.

'*Dear Mother,*' it said,
'*There is nothing to report since I last wrote and I hope you are well too. My great-aunts had an*

*interesting time at the meeting of the Society for the
Prevention of Chimney Smoke this afternoon and I
took exercise with a young uniformed community
on the beach. Your affectionate daughter.'*

'But,' Emma said, holding it up, 'lots of things have
happened since I last wrote. I've been to church and
met the Brownie Pack and I've been in the hospital for
hours and hours and I've been on the swings and in an
ambulance, and we had wonderful races, and I won the
obstacle race with Tewksbury and – and – Tewky is
lost.' She burst into tears.

'I'm sure your mother doesn't want to hear all about
the games you played,' Aunt Aurora said.

'And now what are you crying about?' Aunt Clarice
said, but she did pat Emma on the shoulder.

'Because I've lost my Tewky. I've lost my baby – my
toy puppy.'

'Well, anyway you're too old for a toy like that now so
perhaps it's just as well,' said Aunt Aurora.

'But I'm not too old,' Emma sobbed. 'And I want my
tea and I think you're both horrid, horrid, horrid.'

'Bed with dry bread and water is the best punishment
for such an angry tantrum,' said Aunt Aurora. And
Emma rushed up the stairs, only too glad to throw herself on her bed and go on crying for a bit. Presently
Aunt Clarice came up with a tray.

'I put just a tiny scrape of butter on the bread,' she

whispered as though not wanting great-aunt Aurora to hear. 'And cold milk is just as nasty as cold water so I've given you some instead.' It was all Emma wanted. She ate her tea, undressed, washed, cleaned her teeth, brushed her hair, said her prayers twice, folded up her clothes, and got back into bed and was soon sound asleep.

11 · Postman's knock

Next morning, almost before Emma had time to start worrying about Tewksbury again, she spotted a letter addressed to herself. She whisked it out of the pile the postman had brought. Great-aunt Aurora saw her and wanted to know who it was from. Emma did not recognise the handwriting and said so. The great-aunts made her open it and she read out:

> '*Dear Madam,*
> *We came to the seaside at Cobble yesterday. After the coach had started we noticed that our young toddler Ted was nursing a strange toy. It was sopping wet. Our Betsy thinks he must have trailed it through a rock pool When I came to dry it out at home I found the zipped pocket with a letter in with this address so I am writing to find out if the toy is yours and if I should return it to the same address. It seems like a dog wearing a real baby's suit.*
> *Yours sincerely, Fannie Leaf (Mrs).*'

'Oh, how lovely,' Emma exclaimed, as she finished

reading. 'Tewksbury is safe and Sam didn't hide him after all.'

'Well, you certainly don't want that silly toy back after it's been dragged through a rock pool by somebody else's baby,' said Aunt Aurora.

'Oh, Tewky won't mind a wetting,' Emma said, 'and, how sweet that a dear little baby liked him so much.'

'In that case I suggest you write and say that the baby can keep it,' said Aunt Clarice.

'Daddy wouldn't like that,' Emma said. 'He only bought him for me a little while ago because he wanted me to have him. And even if I didn't love Tewksbury it would be rude to give him away. It shows my prayers have been answered because I prayed hard for him last night.'

'Well, we certainly don't want a nasty wet dirty toy in this house,' said Aunt Aurora.

Emma wrote at once thanking the mother of the toddler and said how pleased she was Tewksbury had been found and that the toddler had liked him, but she would be very glad to see him back as soon as possible. She sent her love to the toddler and to Betsy, hoping she was about her own age. Aunt Clarice read the letter and said she thought it rather silly, but she gave Emma a stamp to put on it and when they went out, let her post it.

From then on whenever the postman came, Emma rushed out hoping he had brought the parcel. She was a little bit afraid that if the great-aunt Aurora got it first she might hide Tewky from her till she went home.

After three days of waiting she was looking hopefully out of an upstairs window for the postman, when she saw him coming down the gangway with a handful of letters but no sign of a parcel. She rushed down the stairs to open the door to him.

'Are you sure there isn't a parcel for me?' she asked him. 'I'm expecting one.'

The postman shook his head. 'Only one letter,' he said, and Emma hoped and hoped it might be from her mother. But it was not in her handwriting. It seemed to be a long thick letter in a light brown envelope, and it looked so dull she was sure it was for one of the great-aunts, till she saw her name on it. The great-aunts heard the postman's voice and came to the door just in time to watch Emma open the letter. Suddenly she gave a squeak of joy. 'It's Tewky back again', she cried. 'Hurrah! hurrah!'

'Don't be so ridiculous,' said Aunt Aurora, 'it's only a letter. You're old enough now not to talk such nonsense all the time.'

But Emma could see the dear pink ears peeping flatly out from behind the short letter from the baby's mother thanking her for hers. She ran upstairs to her room and pulled Tewksbury out. The mother explained that the rags inside him were so wet and bedraggled she was not adding to the postage by sending them. But she had washed and ironed his growy and ironed her mother's letter too.

Emma stuffed Tewksbury out again with all her socks and her pyjamas too, and then zipped him up and gave him a big hug. When she took him down, the great-aunts were amazed to see him back in his old plump form. Emma was so afraid that they would make her put her socks back in the drawer and her pyjamas under her pillow, that she just kept on talking about what a lovely day it was. And then suddenly something wonderful happened. First there was a knock on the door. Great-aunt Aurora went, and came back with a yellow letter.

'It's a telegram,' she said. Then she looked at it more closely and said, 'Good gracious, it's addressed to Emma. I never heard of a child receiving a telegram before. Two letters in one day!'

Emma was so pleased to have Tewksbury back she could hardly believe there was anything left that could be nicer, but when she opened it, she found there was.

LOVELY FAT BABY BROTHER BORN FOR YOU LAST NIGHT. FETCHING YOU TODAY LOVE DADDY.'

Now Emma jumped up and down in her excitement and threw Tewksbury in the air and how ever much the great-aunts said 'don't,' 'don't,' 'don't', she shouted again and again. 'It's a boy! It's a boy! It's a boy! I've got a lovely fat brother.'

'I had better go and pack for you,' said Aunt Clarice, 'if you are leaving today.'

'I can pack for myself,' Emma said. 'Please don't bother. Packing is one of the things we learn in Brownies for our Brownie road.' The great-aunts took no notice.

She was overjoyed to see her father again! Everything wonderful seemed to happen at once. Now she had Tewksbury back, she was going home, her father was holding her suitcase in one hand and her hand in the other and soon she was going to be back with her mother and was going to see her own fat baby brother.

'I don't care how ugly he is,' Emma said, 'or how boring to start with, I just love him, love him, love him.' But when Emma crept into her mother's room and saw the new baby in her arms, he did not seem the least bit

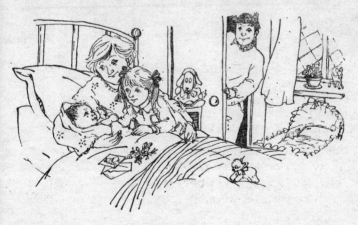

ugly and certainly not boring. He was opening his mouth in a big yawn, something that even Tewksbury could never really do. Emma held one finger up and although her brother was not yet a day old, he somehow managed to wrap his own fingers round it very tightly.

'I think he's saying, "Don't go away. Please stay,"' Emma said.

12 · Name this child

Now that Emma was home the first thing she had to do was to tell Sam that Tewksbury was safe and to say she was sorry she thought he had hidden him. Sam was very surprised to see her.

'I thought you would have to stay in hospital for weeks,' he said. 'Sassy and I were going to come and see you on visitors' day, and if they didn't let children come in she was going to sit on my shoulders and we were going to put one of our Mum's frocks right over both of us so we looked like one very tall person.'

At Brownies, on Saturday, there was a great deal for Emma to tell in the pow-wow ring. She decided only to tell the nice things and the exciting things, and not to go on about the stuffiness of her great-aunts. She told about meeting the Brownie Pack and the sports and winning the obstacle race and the playground, and said her fall was all her own fault for not obeying Packy's call to follow her and then for not being wide awake to climbing safely. She tried to make losing Tewksbury sound funny and not awful. She told the Brownies how wonderful the doll's house looked in the children's ward and how lovely it was playing with it, and then she told them how Tewksbury came back, just like a letter, and had to be filled out again, and last of all she told the great news of her baby brother.

'And soon we shall have the great news of Tawny's baby,' said Amanda. 'You will promise to let us know at once whether it's a boy or a girl, won't you Tawny?'

'I'll ask Monster John to give it out in church the next Sunday,' Tawny said.

'But supposing it's born on a Monday?' 'We can't wait as long as that.'

'Oh, please tell him to tell us before that. Will you ask him to put a flag out on the rectory gate when it's born?' 'But then we shan't know whether it's a boy or a girl.'

Suddenly Amanda had an idea.

'Couldn't Monster John put a blue ribbon on the rectory gate if it's a boy and a pink ribbon if it's a girl?' she said.

Tawny said she would ask him to do this, and the Brownies said they would give him the ribbons as soon as they could go to the shop so that he would have them all ready.

From then, day after day, one or other of the Brownies, or even two or three, went out of their way on their walk to school and home again to have a look at the rectory gate. They also went on their way to and from

Brownies. Tawny had not been to Brownies for a little while.

Emma, Sassy and Tulip were on their way to Brownies when Sassy said:

'Let's just go and have a look at the rectory gate.' So they all went and there, at last, was the ribbon they had bought.

'But it's *all* the ribbon,' Tulip said. 'We only meant him to put pink or blue.'

'And he's put pink *and* blue. What can it mean? I expect he forgot and was so excited he put both.'

'I've just had an idea,' said Tulip. 'If he's put blue and he's put pink it must mean there's a boy and a girl. It must mean Tawny's had twins.'

'Oh, how lovely.' 'We never thought of twins!' 'But we've only knitted enough things for one baby.'

'Tewksbury will be very glad to lend his growy for one of them,' said Emma.

The Brownies raced up the hill to the Brownie barn to tell Brown Owl that Tawny must have had two babies but Brown Owl knew already.

'Yes,' she said, 'it really is twins.'

'And we've never had twins before in the Pack,' Sassy said. 'Except me and I'm only half of twins.'

'I hope Tawny's twins won't be quite so terrible as Sassy and Sam,' Lucinda said.

'I'm not terrible any more,' said Sassy.

'And nor is Sam,' said Emma. 'He was very kind to

me when I fell off the climbing tower. Nobody but Sam would have thought of sending for an ambulance for me. If Tawny's twins are as nice as Sassy and Sam they'll be all right.'

When they had settled down Brown Owl said, 'And now what is our next Venture going to be?' The Brownies had taken their V badges off once everything was ready for Tawny and some had put them on again for small Ventures. Now they were longing to do another whole Pack Venture together.

'A long time ago we had a wonderful Pack Venture of getting ready for Tawny's wedding,' said Angela. 'Can't we now have a Venture of getting ready for a beautiful christening for Emma's baby brother and the twins?'

'We shall have to ask their mothers and fathers if they would like it,' said Brown Owl. 'It does sound a lovely idea.'

'Well, would I be able to come,' asked Joey, 'because I've never been christened?'

'We all went to Tawny's wedding and none of us had been married,' Sassy reminded her.

'Perhaps Monster John would christen you too,' said Emma. 'People can be christened when they're quite old can't they Brown Owl?'

'Certainly, even grown-ups can be christened,' Brown Owl said. 'Nowadays grown-ups are often christened and Confirmed at the same service.'

Just before Brownies ended Monster John came in himself in case nobody had seen the ribbons on the gate. He told them all about the twins and how heavy they were and how beautiful, and how pleased and happy and well Tawny was. He was very pleased with all the offers of extra baby clothes the Brownies made, and especially Emma's, as Tawny had only expected one baby.

Then they told him how lovely it would be if all three babies could be christened at once as well as Joey, and he said he would talk to Tawny and to Emma's and Joey's mothers about it.

'We could have a wonderful christening party in the Brownie barn like we did after your marriage to Tawny,' Tulip said, 'with a huge christening cake.'

'We could make coconut kisses.' 'And Melting Moments.' 'And an iced hedgehog.' 'And lots and lots of lemon squash and tea.' The Brownies all started to speak at once. 'And flowers on the table.' 'And flowers by the door.' 'And we promise we'll make your favourite kind of sandwiches, Monster John.'

Monster John said the party after a christening was a very nice thing to have as it made everybody get to know each other and was all part of the celebration. But the christening itself was the important part. Some babies were christened without parties. A very ill baby could be christened in a tiny basin of water by anybody who was there – his mother or father or nurse. Christenings in church at a family service were the best because it was like opening the door of the church to a new member. That was why the font was usually near the main door of the church.

'Well, anyway,' said Jean, 'we can learn to sing a special christening hymn.'

'What shall our baby's christian name be?' Emma asked her mother, at home.

'What would you like?' her mother asked her.

'Tewky has such a lot of grand names that I think, this time, as it's a christian name I would choose a nice plain James,' said Emma.

'Like Daddy?'

'Yes, but you always call him Jim, so we'd easily know the difference.'

'I can't think of any name I'd like more,' Emma's mother said. 'If Daddy agrees.'

And he did.

'So James it is to be,' Emma's mother said, very pleased.

Monster John and Tawny took longer to decide what to call the twins. Some days they were George and Georgiana and some days they were Augustus and Gertrude, but mostly they were just Jack and Jill.

Joey's mother said she could add another name to Josephine if she liked. She would have liked a pony's name like Firefly or Merrylegs but in the end she looked at a picture of a wild rose, her favourite flower, and chose the name 'Rose'.

13 · A christening bunch

All the parents agreed it was a beautiful idea to have all three babies and Joey christened together. Joey's mother said that her father had been abroad when Joey was born and she had waited till he came back for her christening and then, somehow, when he came back it was forgotten. Monster John said forgetting God's blessings was much easier than refusing them and much more usual too. But God never got tired of giving blessings so it was never too late to be christened. So the christening was planned for next Sunday afternoon.

'There's not nearly so long to wait for the christening day as there was for the wedding day,' said Joey. 'But there's still a whole week.'

'A week's only just enough to learn our new music,' said Jean.

As all the Brownies were also in the church choir, they were going to wear their white surplices over their Brownie uniforms for the christening, just as they had done on the wedding day, and then change afterwards to re-appear as Brownies. They helped to wash and iron their surplices. Tulip and Sassy helped Tawny to get the twins' christening clothes ready. One was more silky than the other but both were covered in fine embroidery and lace.

'Mind you don't scorch my christening clothes,' warned Monster John. 'I haven't forgotten Sassy's iron-shaped patch in my wedding shirt.'

'Which one of these did you wear when you were christened, Monster John?' Tulip asked.

'Both. One on the top of the other. They called this beautiful thing a petticoat,' he said. 'All the babies wore them under their dresses in my baby days.'

'It's lucky they did,' said Tawny. 'Now we've got twins, one can wear the dress and the other the petticoat.'

'But which?' asked Sassy.

'Well, we can't put a boy in a petticoat nowadays, so he'll have to wear the dress.' So Sassy threaded the blue ribbon from the gate through the little slots in the dress and Tulip threaded the pink through the lace on the petticoat.

Emma helped her mother to wash and iron James' flowery christening robe. (It was the one that Tewksbury had slipped out of into the bird-bath.)

Joey said she would like to be christened in Brownie uniform.

The Brownies swept and dusted the church themselves and decorated it with flowers from the cornfields.

They put red poppies and blue scabious and white ox-eyed daisies in jars at the ends of the pews and moss round the bottom of the font with scarlet pimpernels and blue speedwells tucked into it. It was a very old font with a lid like a steeple that had to be lifted with a pulley. Monster John pulled it up all ready for the christening and the Brownies helped him to get the water ready that would remind everybody of the promise between God and the godparents to protect the four new Christian souls from the horrible things in the world that could make them bad.

'Jesus loves little children, doesn't he, Monster John?' Angela said with a contented sigh. 'He took them in his arms and blessed them.'

For godparents, the twins were going to have Tawny's brother and some cousins of hers and Monster

John's. James was going to have two friends of his father's from work and his mother's sister. Joey was going to have Amanda's father for her godfather and, for godmothers, Sassy's mother and Brown Owl.

The christening was part of the Sunday afternoon Evensong service. Everybody turned round to face the font and the parents and godparents stood round it, three of them holding babies. Joey stood with them.

Monster John began the christening by talking about 'these children' and the godparents made their three-fold promise all together.

Then Monster John took James and held him in one arm and with his free hand dipped a little shell into the font and poured from it a little trickle of water over the baby's head. Even the Brownies who were not tall enough to see it all, could hear him say: 'James, I baptise you in the name of the Father, the Son and the Holy Spirit.' They could hear the water trickling back into the font and they could hear the roar that James let out, and his cries turning suddenly to a coo of pleasure as Monster John lit a candle for him. They could see the glow of the candle as he handed it to the baby's father, who carried it back to his pew, still lit. They knew that he would light it for his son every year on his christening day to remind him of the darkness being driven out by God's love.

Then Monster John began on the twins.

'Name this child,' he said, and Tawny's brother

answered 'Justin' for the first, and later Monster John's cousin answered 'Christina' for the second. He lit a candle for each twin and left them shining on the edge of the font till he could carry them both back up the church himself.

Then Joey came and stood by the font. She could just see over the top of it into the water.

'Josephine Rose,' Monster John said as she bent her head over the font so that he could sprinkle some water on to it, 'I baptise you in the name of the Father, the Son and the Holy Spirit.' He made the sign of the cross on her forehead too as she was received into the church. He lit a candle for Joey, and her father carried it for her as they went back to their pew together.

Then came the thanking and the singing and, last of all, the blessing for everybody, before they went out into the world again to be, as Emma whispered to her father hopefully, 'shining lights of love and kindness'.

As it was such a lovely day, the christening party was held in the little wood near the Brownie barn. Under the trees the babies' prams rocked softly in the breeze.

On the long table stood the big cake that Amanda's mother had made for all three babies and Joey. It was covered with white icing that she had pulled up with a knife into crisp little peaks. On the top were three sugar cradles with three babies in them and a chocolate doll that looked very much like Joey in Brownie uniform. Two of the cradles had blue sugar pillows and one had pink.

The Brownies had made Monster John's favourite kinds of sandwiches. They and their mothers had made all their very best party food. And there were pink and white sugared almonds scattered all over the table among the daisy heads and trailing wild convolvulus.

Monster John was right about everybody getting to know each other. The godparents who had come specially for the christening soon made friends with everybody and it was like one great big family party. When tea was over nobody wanted to go home, except the babies who soon began to yell for their share in the feast. It was odd, Emma thought, that the noise no longer sounded like a cog-wheel that needed oiling. To her, now, it was more like somebody asking quite politely for some tea.

Emma helped her mother to push the pram down the hill after the party. Her brother was sound asleep. Everybody was happy. When they reached home Emma hurried in to lay out baby James's nightie and sleeping things and put out a clean nappy and everything for his last wash. While her mother was changing James, Emma helped her father to bring the pram into the hall. She sat down to watch her mother getting the baby ready for his feed before she put him down to bed. Emma picked Tewksbury up and put him on her knees.

'Don't think I'm too old for you, Tewky,' she said, 'or that I don't love you any more. But now we know that you can win an obstacle race for me and get yourself sent home by post it shows you're not a baby any more. In fact you're just the sort of thing a baby brother would like to have for a friend.' And she sat Tewksbury up at the foot end of the cot all ready for when the baby grew big enough to want to play with him.

'I'm very glad Tawny had twins,' Emma told her mother. 'But I think I'm glad we have just got James. I can see he's going to take up quite a lot of time to look after even with me to help you. We certainly wouldn't have had time for a live dog as well. But Tewky's just right.'

Knight has a whole range of paperbacks for boys and girls, from mystery, adventure and crime to fantasy, animal stories and factual books on sport and other activities for the holidays.

If you have enjoyed this book, why not try some of those listed on the following pages?

VERILY ANDERSON

The Brownies and their Animal Friends

Amanda and her Brownie Friends decide to have an animal quest – and the results amaze even Brown Owl. But the Brownies' love and experience of animals is very useful when they are asked to provide a special item of entertainment at a festival. A festival which is more exciting than anyone could have guessed.

KNIGHT BOOKS

VERILY ANDERSON

The Brownies' Day Abroad

The Brownies go to France for the day – which would have been perfect if it hadn't been for the terrible twins, Sassy and Sam. But even so the Brownies agree that all their hard work earning the money to go was worthwhile. And they hold a special French Day on their return to show their families what they have learned abroad.

Brownie Cook Book

Lots of recipes for Brownies of any age. This book has hints on helping in the kitchen and the tools you will need for your own cooking as well as a step-by-step guide for making short-bread, pancakes, meringues and many other tempting dishes.

KNIGHT BOOKS

OTFRIED PREUSSLER

The Robber Hotzenplotz

The wicked robber Hotzenplotz was the terror
of the village. Whatever he wanted he stole
and he was always armed with a sword, a
pistol and seven knives. Then he took Grandmother's musical coffee mill and Kasperl and
Seppel just had to do something about it. But
the ingenious plan misfired and when robber
Hotzenplotz captured them both, there
seemed no way of disentangling themselves
from such a fix.

KNIGHT BOOKS

OTFRIED PREUSSLER

The Further Adventures of The Robber Hotzenplotz

The robber Hotzenplotz escaped from prison, still as wicked as ever. And something just had to be done about it, so off went Kasperl and Seppel to trap him. Then everything went sadly wrong and he kidnapped Grandmother and captured them both too. All seemed lost until a crocodile-dog called Fido arrived on the scene and justice triumphed once again.

KNIGHT BOOKS

OTFRIED PREUSSLER

The Final Adventures of
The Robber Hotzenplotz

'I don't suppose you'll believe me,' he said,
'but I really have made up my mind to be
honest in future! On my word as a robber, I
have!'

Hotzenplotz sets out to prove his honesty
but only Kasperl and Seppel become con-
vinced. Widow Petunia Shuttlecock's crystal
ball goes missing; Grandmother loses two of
her prize pumpkins and everyone suspects
Hotzenplotz. So upset is he that he runs away
to search for honest work. But Fido, the
crocodile dog, Kasperl and Seppel chase after
him . . .

KNIGHT BOOKS

B.B.

The Forest of Boland Light Railway

The Forest of Boland Light Railway, with its magnificent steam engine, the Boland Belle, is the pride and joy of the gnomes who live in the forest. But one day their enemies the leprechauns overcome the gnomes in a surprise attack, and drag them off to their stronghold, Castle Shera. The outlook seems bleak, but the cowzies come to the rescue just in time.

The Wizard of Boland

The gnomes of the Forest of Boland are horrified to find a dragon sleeping in a cave near their village; but the wicked Wizard Homm is delighted to see the same dragon browsing among the willows in the forest because he needs some dragon's blood to work his best spells. But the Wizard's greed is his downfall . . .

KNIGHT BOOKS

KNIGHT BOOKS

Verily Anderson

Otfried Preussler

'BB'

All these books are available at your local bookshop or newsagent, or can be ordered direct from the publisher. Just tick the titles you want and fill in the form below.

Prices and availability subject to change without notice.

CORONET BOOKS, P.O. Box 11, Falmouth, Cornwall.

Please send cheque or postal order, and allow the following for postage and packing:

U.K. — One book 22p plus 10p per copy for each additional book ordered, up to a maximum of 82p.

B.F.P.O. and EIRE — 22p for the first book plus 10p per copy for the next 6 books, thereafter 4p per book.

OTHER OVERSEAS CUSTOMERS — 30p for the first book and 10p per copy for each additional book.

Name ....

Address ....

....